"I swear to tell the truth, the whole truth, and nothing but the—"

"Quiet, Wishbone," Ellen said. "Joe, Wishbone has made a total mess. He's in big trouble. I want you to put him on the back porch—now."

Wishbone sprang up on all fours. "Hey, what kind of trial is this? You can't just sentence me. Where's your evidence? What about witnesses? And when do I get to testify?"

Joe sighed and moved toward Wishbone. "Sorry, boy," he said softly.

"I demand justice! This is the United States of America!" Wishbone jumped off the chair. "Wait a minute! What happened to liberty and justice for all?"

The Adventures of **WiSHBONe**™ titles in Large-Print Editions:

The Adventures of WISHBONE™

A TALE OF TWO SITTERS

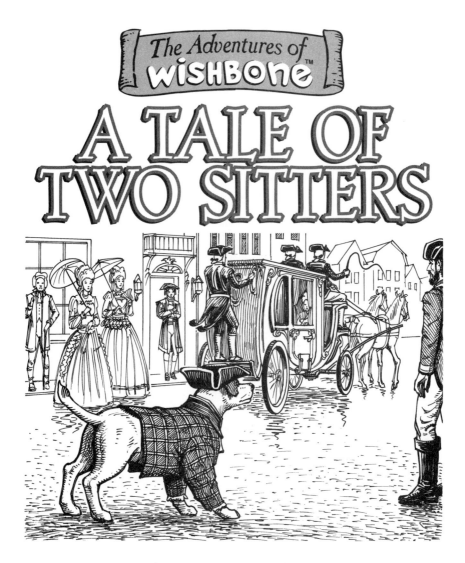

by Joanne Barkan
Based on the teleplay by Stephanie Simpson
Inspired by *A Tale of Two Cities*
by Charles Dickens

WISHBONE™ created by Rick Duffield

Gareth Stevens Publishing
MILWAUKEE

This book is a work of fiction. The characters, incidents, and dialogues are products of the author's imagination and are not to be construed as real. Any resemblance to actual events or persons, living or dead, is entirely coincidental.

For a free color catalog describing Gareth Stevens' list of high-quality books and multimedia programs, call 1-800-542-2595 (USA) or 1-800-461-9120 (Canada). Gareth Stevens Publishing's Fax: (414) 225-0377.

Library of Congress Cataloging-in-Publication Data

Barkan, Joanne.
    A tale of two sitters / by Joanne Barkan.
        p. cm.
    Originally published: Allen, Texas; Big Red Chair Books, © 1998.
    (The adventures of Wishbone; #9)
        Summary: When David enlists Joe's aid in babysitting, Wishbone escapes
    from his noisy home and imagines himself as Charles Darnay, a young Frenchman
    who, despite great danger, returns to France during the Revolution to help a friend.
        ISBN 0-8368-2305-2 (lib. bdg.)
        [1. Dogs—Fiction. 2. France—History—Revolution, 1789-1799—Fiction.
    3. Friendship—Fiction.] I. Dickens, Charles, 1812-1870. Tale of two cities.
    II. Title. III. Series: Adventures of Wishbone; #9.
    PZ7.B25039Tal   1999
    [Fic]—dc21   98-47166

This edition first published in 1999 by
Gareth Stevens Publishing
1555 North RiverCenter Drive, Suite 201
Milwaukee, Wisconsin 53212 USA

© 1998 Big Feats! Entertainment. First published by Big Red Chair Books™,
a Division of Lyrick Publishing™, 300 E. Bethany Drive, Allen, Texas 75002.

Edited by Pam Pollack
Copy edited by Jonathon Brodman
Cover design by Lyle Miller
Interior illustrations by Don Punchatz
Wishbone illustration on page 155 by Laine Miller
Wishbone photograph by Carol Kaelson

WISHBONE, the **Wishbone** portrait, and the Big Feats! Entertainment logo are trademarks and service marks of Big Feats! Entertainment.

Printed in the United States of America

1 2 3 4 5 6 7 8 9 03 02 01 00 99

To Jon R. Friedman,

with whom it's always been

the best of times

FROM THE BIG RED CHAIR . . .

Oh . . . hi! Wishbone here. You caught me right in the middle
of some of my favorite things—books. Let me welcome you to
THE ADVENTURES OF WISHBONE. In each of these books, I have
adventures with my friends in Oakdale and imagine myself as a
character in one of the greatest stories of all time. This story takes
place in the spring, when Joe is twelve and he and his friends are
in the sixth grade—during the first season of my television show.
In *A TALE OF TWO SITTERS,* I imagine I'm Charles Darnay, a
young Frenchman from Charles Dickens's great novel *A TALE OF
TWO CITIES.* It is a story about honor, justice, and Charles's
narrow escape during the terror of the French Revolution.
You're in for a real treat, so pull up a chair and a snack and
enjoy *A TALE OF TWO SITTERS!*

Chapter One

Wishbone stood at the top of the stairs, his tail wagging. His white, short-haired coat shone in the morning light. Even the black patch on his back, the velvety brown right ear, and the brown ring around his left eye reflected the bright sun. He sniffed the air.

Yes, it is the best of times! he thought. *Saturday! Breakfast in my stomach, lunch and dinner still to come, and a whole day to run around, dig, snack—and play with Joe!* Wishbone glanced down the stairs into the living room. *By the way—where is Joe?* He sniffed again. *Oh, he's still in his bedroom.*

Wishbone turned and bounded toward Joe's room. "Let's go, slowpoke! Time to hit the streets. Just you and me, Joe. A dog and his boy. Searching for adventure!"

Wishbone trotted through the bedroom doorway. Twelve-year-old Joe Talbot sat on the edge of his bed. He was dressed in jeans and a brown plaid shirt, and was holding a single black sneaker. He looked annoyed.

Wishbone's dark eyes darted from the sneaker in Joe's hand to the white sweat socks on Joe's feet. The matching sneaker was nowhere to be seen. "Now, here's a problem that I can solve in a jiffy. Boy's best friend to the rescue! Right, Joe?"

Joe didn't answer.

Wishbone sighed. "Nobody ever listens to the dog. As usual, my actions will have to speak louder than my words."

Wishbone stretched out his two front legs, lowered his head, and scrambled under the bed. A few seconds later, he scrambled out with the matching black sneaker in his mouth. He dropped the shoe next to Joe's left foot.

"*Voilà!* That's French for 'here it is!'"

Joe grinned. "Thanks, Wishbone!" he said. "You're the best." He pulled on his sneakers, tied the laces, and headed for the door. "Race you downstairs!" he called over his shoulder.

Wishbone leaped toward the door. "You're on!"

Joe's sneakers pounded down the carpeted stairs. Wishbone's paws pattered at top speed. Joe's straight brown hair bounced up and down. Wishbone's floppy V-shaped ears did the same. Three pairs of feet reached the bottom step at almost the same moment.

Wishbone did a quick somersault. "The race is mine— by a nose!"

"Where's the fire, guys?" a voice called out.

Wishbone and Joe looked toward the sound of the voice. Joe smiled. His mom, Ellen Talbot, stood in the kitchen doorway, her eyes sparkling with amusement. She was wearing a heavy wool jacket and had a leather backpack slung over one shoulder. She jangled a set of car keys in one hand.

"Joe, I'm going out to run some errands, but I'll be back this afternoon."

"Okay," Joe said.

"Do you want to go to the park later on?" Ellen asked.

"Sure."

Wishbone's ears perked up upon hearing Ellen's remark. "Don't forget to invite the dog."

Ellen glanced in the hall mirror and straightened the narrow headband that held back her medium-length, wavy brown hair. "What's your plan for this morning?"

"David's coming over," Joe answered. David Barnes was one of Joe's two best friends. He was also the top science student and inventor in their class at school. "He built this brand-new remote-control car, and we're going to test it to see how it works."

Wishbone's jaw dropped open. He panted. "Cool! Can I drive? Can I? Think of it as part of my overall training. Everyone needs a little driver's ed."

Ellen gave Joe a quick hug. "That sounds neat. I'd like to see it when I get back." She bent down and rubbed the top of Wishbone's head. "Have fun, guys."

Wishbone's eyelids half closed with pleasure. "Nice, Ellen. Just a little lower, and to the left."

"'Bye, Mom," Joe called as his mother was closing the front door. He picked up a basketball magazine that was lying on the coffee table in the living room and sat down on the couch. Wishbone jumped onto the couch and sat beside him.

"Listen, Joe, how about a walk, followed by a snack? Then after that we could have a game of Frisbee, followed by a snack, and then some digging, and we'll follow that up with a snack—not necessarily in that order. In fact, now's probably a good time for the first snack. One of those doggie ginger snaps would hit the spot. You know—the blue box under the—"

The doorbell rang.

"Who is it?" Joe called out.

The door opened. A boy with short, dark curly hair and dark skin leaned inside. "It's me—David."

Joe looked up at the door. "Come on in. Did you bring the car?"

Wishbone hopped down from the couch and trotted over toward David. "*This* I've got to see."

9

In one hand, David held a squat, rectangular vehicle made of many small metal parts. The car had four wide wheels with thick black-rubber treads, and a small steering wheel. A Daredevil Dan action figure sat in the driver's seat. A tall metal antenna rose from the back end of the car. In his other hand, David held the remote-control unit—a small black box with another tall antenna.

Wishbone sniffed the car. "Excellent, David! This model meets all my specifications."

David hurried into the living room. "There's just one small problem," he said to Joe in a low voice. "I have to baby-sit."

Joe looked stunned. "You have to *what?*"

David pointed toward the front door. Wishbone took a few steps in that direction and stopped short. *Uh-oh. I thought I smelled trouble a couple of seconds ago. Now I'm looking at it!*

Emily Barnes, David's five-year-old sister, stood in the hallway. Wishbone backed up. With her sweet smile, big brown eyes, and dark curly hair tied neatly into two pigtails, she looked angelic.

Ha! Looks can be deceiving, Wishbone thought. He took two more cautious steps backward. *Once she tried to dress me in her ballerina tutu. Then there was the bubble-bath incident. I want out of here!*

"Hi, Wishbone," Emily said sweetly. "Say hello to Tina."

Wishbone took another step back. "Tina? Who's Tina?"

A second five-year-old girl stepped into the hallway. She had almond-shaped eyes, long, straight black hair pulled back in a ponytail, and a smile as sweet as Emily's. "Hi, Wishbone," she cooed.

Two of them, one of me—not good. I'm outnumbered. Okay, try not to look cute, and they'll leave you alone. Wishbone turned quickly and scrambled back to the couch, his nails clicking on the wood floor.

David looked nervous. "Joe, this is Emily's friend, Tina."

"You mean you're baby-sitting for *both* of them?" Joe asked.

David nodded. "Well, I was kind of thinking that, you know, maybe you could sort of help me baby-sit."

"Sort of help you baby-sit?" Joe echoed.

Wishbone nodded. *Two-on-two is a better baby-sitting ratio. There's strength in numbers. You need that to keep their kind under control.*

"Look, Joe," David said, "let's go ahead and do what we planned to do. Emily and Tina will stay out of the way. Right, girls?"

Emily and Tina looked at each other and smiled.

"Wrong, David." Wishbone lay down and covered his eyes with his paws. He moaned. "It's the worst of times. It's the winter of despair!"

David motioned for Joe to follow him. "Come on," he said. "Let's go test the car outside."

Joe grinned. "Great—let's do it!"

"Come on, girls," David called to Emily and Tina. "We're going outside."

Wishbone sprang up as Joe and David headed for the door. "We're back on track. It's the best of times! It's the spring of hope!"

Emily pursed her lips and shook her head. "No. We want to stay inside."

Tina nodded. "Inside," she said firmly.

Joe rolled his eyes. David groaned. Wishbone sighed and walked slowly to the coffee table. With another sigh, he rested his chin on the edge of the table.

"Well, here we go again. The best of times, the worst of times . . . spring of hope, winter of despair. Hmm . . . why do those words sound so familiar? Wait—I remember!"

They're from a famous novel called *A Tale of Two Cities*, by the English writer Charles Dickens. The book was first published in 1859. Dickens called it "the best story I have written."

A Tale of Two Cities really does take place in two cities—London, England; and Paris, France. The hero, Charles Darnay, really does live through both the best of times and the worst of times. It was the age of the French Revolution, in the late eighteenth century, when the people of France turned their entire world upside down.

Chapter Two

Wishbone pictured the city of Paris in the year 1780. In his mind, he saw elegant avenues, luxurious palaces, and huge public squares decorated with statues of the kings of France. He saw the massive towers of the Notre Dame cathedral and the gilded church dome next to the hospital called Les Invalides. He also saw shabby alleyways lined with small, dark houses, and grim stone fortresses used as prisons.

Wishbone imagined himself as Charles Darnay, a young and honorable Frenchman. Darnay was about to be swept into a whirlwind of events far beyond his control.

Charles Darnay nudged open the front door of the Paris rooming house with his nose. It was almost noon. He hopped down the single wood step to the street.

Well, that place was all right for one night, he thought. *It wasn't the Versailles palace, but it wasn't a flea bag, either.*

The thought of fleas made Darnay give himself a quick scratch under one floppy ear. He sniffed the late-morning air. His tail wagged.

No summer storms today, and it's not too hot for a walk. I have exactly two hours before my hired coach leaves Paris for my uncle's château—his castle in the country.

Charles gazed down a wide boulevard that led to the Louvre palace. The gold-painted carriages of the aristocrats—members of the ruling families of France—rolled toward the formal gardens and park surrounding the palace. Noblemen dressed in embroidered satin jackets, brocade waistcoats, and silk knee breeches lounged inside the carriages on velvet cushions. Footmen in white, powdered wigs and long lace cuffs perched on steps on the sides of the carriages. They were ready to jump down and fling open the doors on command. The drivers snapped their whips above the heads of the high-stepping horses.

Women of the royal court wore hoop skirts the size of tents. They carried taffeta parasols to shield themselves from the sun. They strolled with their servants, their admirers, and their admirers' servants. The women wore powdered

wigs that resembled mountains of ringlets and curls. On top of the wigs, hats of every imaginable shape sprouted plumes and bows. Jeweled walking sticks and gold-encrusted canes glinted in the sunlight. The breeze carried the scent of rich perfumes and expensive tobacco.

Charles sneezed. "I'm allergic to those people," he muttered. "They're a bad breed—selfish and cruel."

He turned his tail on the scene and walked briskly in the direction of Saint Antoine, the district of the working-class poor people. As he made his way, the streets soon became narrow and were filled with peddlers, beggars, and children wearing only rags. They shouted and sang and called to one another. Charles slowed down. His black nose twitched.

I smell garlic, stale bread, old wine—and even older cheese, he thought. *Magnifique! Wonderful!* He sniffed several more times and sighed. *I'm afraid the smells of fear, anger, and hatred are stronger than anything else in Saint Antoine.*

Women carrying cloth bundles and crying infants made their way among the crudely built wagons and carts. Charles's nails clicked on the cobblestones, which had been laid every which way. He scrambled across a particularly uneven patch as he tried to avoid bumping into a blind man who was carrying a heavy load of straw.

"*Excusez-moi,*" Charles said politely. "Pardon me."

As he turned to watch the man, Charles caught sight of a massive four-hundred-year-old fortress at the far end of the street.

"The Bastille!" he exclaimed.

A shiver ran down his back from his shoulders to the tip of his tail. His fur bristled. Like everyone else, he knew that the most powerful aristocrats in France had their enemies thrown into the Bastille prison without first allowing them to have a trial before a judge. Once locked inside, few ever left the miserable, cold dungeons of the Bastille alive. Most prisoners died alone and in despair. For Charles, the Bastille represented everything that was cruel and unfair about the rule of the aristocrats in France.

The sight of it is enough to turn any warm-blooded person cold! Charles thought. "A-choo!"

Once again he turned his tail on the scene. He hurried down another side street, which opened up into a small square. Simple shops lined the square, and an ancient stone fountain stood in the middle. As Charles crossed the square, his ears picked up a distant sound—a low, thundering noise. Soon the sound grew louder, more pounding, more frantic.

Others in the square noticed it. Heads turned. The low thundering turned into a hammering noise. It echoed up and down the canyonlike streets. Charles recognized the sound—the iron shoes of galloping horses slamming against cobblestones.

Charles cried out a warning. "It's a carriage. Get out of the way!"

A team of six gray horses swept around a corner and headed directly toward the square. They pulled a large carriage whose huge wheels skimmed over the rough pavement. The driver, high in his seat, snapped his whip again and again.

A shudder passed through the crowd. Children screamed as their parents pushed them to safety. Men and women hurled themselves to the sides of the square. Some rolled on the ground or tried to flatten themselves against the walls of the buildings. With a loud howl, Charles sprang toward the doorway of a wine shop. He squeezed himself into the small space between one doorpost and the legs of a hefty woman who seemed transfixed by the scene. She remained perfectly still, holding up her knitting needles and wool, as if she had suddenly turned to stone.

Charles watched in horror as the carriage swooped into the square. The horses leaped forward, but the carriage lurched unexpectedly and swerved. The horses reared. The driver lost his balance, yelled, then reined in the startled team. The carriage stopped.

"My son!" screamed a tall, thin man dressed in a threadbare shirt and torn leather breeches. "My son!"

He threw himself under the carriage and grasped at something lying between the front wheels and the stamping hooves. Two footmen jumped down from their perches and grabbed the tall, thin man's shoulders. He shook them off and then stood up slowly. In his arms he cradled a limp form—the body of a small boy.

The man threw back his head and shrieked, "Dead!"

Charles saw the blue-velvet curtain that covered the carriage window jerk open. The passenger's head, topped by a powdered wig, turned to look at the crowd. The shocked and hushed crowd stared back at the long, proud face of a man about sixty years old. His pale skin was still smooth, his small nostrils flared slightly, his thin mouth turned down.

Charles gasped. His fur stood on end. His four legs quaked. "It's my uncle—the Marquis Saint Evrémonde!"

The woman standing next to Charles turned and glared down at him. "The marquis—your uncle!" She clutched her knitting so tightly that the knuckles of her reddened hands turned white.

Charles didn't notice her. His eyes were fixed on the carriage. The tall, thin man holding the child shrieked again, "Dead! My child is dead!"

The marquis asked one of his footmen coldly, "Why is he making that horrible noise?"

"It's his child," the footman said in a flat voice.

The marquis's face showed no expression. He took out a black-satin coin purse and glanced at the crowd. "It is extraordinary to me," he said, "that you people cannot take care of yourselves and your children. One or the other of you

17

is forever in the way. Who knows what harm you have done to my horses?"

The marquis turned to the footman and tossed him a gold coin.

"Here," the marquis said, "give it to that man." He leaned back inside the carriage.

The footman threw the coin in the direction of the tall, thin man. Then he quickly climbed back to his perch. The carriage rolled forward.

Charles lifted a paw and started to step out of the doorway. He noticed a tiny object—the gold coin—whiz through the air and through the open window of the carriage.

"Halt!"

It was the voice of the marquis.

The marquis leaned out to look at the spot where he had last seen the tall, thin man and his dead son. They were gone. He then glanced at the crowd—their silent hatred filled the air.

"You vermin," the marquis said to the crowd in a controlled voice. "If I knew which rascal threw that coin into the carriage, I would have him crushed under its wheels. I would ride over any of you very willingly and rid you from the earth."

At the crack of the driver's whip, the horses lunged forward. The carriage sped out of the square.

Charles heard someone growling—a deep, menacing growl. He looked around, then shook himself hard. "It's me growling," he muttered.

"*Monsieur,* your uncle is the Marquis Saint Evrémonde? May I ask Your Excellency what, exactly, is *your* name?"

Charles peered up at the large woman who stood over him, knitting. Her features were strong, but perfectly still. She wore a brightly patterned cloth wrapped around her head, and large earrings. Her knitting needles danced back and forth, although her dark eyes never left Charles's face.

She seemed to be memorizing every one of his markings, every bit of fur, every whisker.

I wouldn't want to get tangled up in her *knitting!* Charles thought. *Could she be a spy?*

Thousands of spies were working all over France—some were employed by the French king, some by the English king, and others by opposing groups of aristocrats.

"*Monsieur,* are you an Evrémonde?" the knitting woman asked.

She's not a spy, Charles thought. *She hates my breed. And why shouldn't she? I am ashamed of my entire family line—and angered by their unfair deeds!*

Charles turned away without answering her. His four sturdy legs carried him quickly across the cobblestones, but his mind remained fixed on the terrible scene that had just occurred in the square. He didn't hear the last words of the knitting woman, although she spoke them clearly.

"I, Madame Defarge, do swear today that I will not rest until every Evrémonde—down to the very last child—has been exterminated from the earth!"

Chapter Three

Charles Darnay sat by himself on the worn leather seat of the hired coach as it bounced along the dusty road. He stretched out his two front legs as far as he could and arched his furred back to relieve the stiff muscles.

It's been six hours since we left Paris, he thought. *I could use a good stretch—and a private moment with a tree. But it's just a few more miles to the village and the château.*

Charles looked out the window and inspected the passing landscape in the crimson light of the setting sun. He stared so intently that his silky, white whiskers quivered.

How lovely the French countryside is—and how miserable! The peasants are being taxed to death by the aristocrats. They don't have enough food to eat, and they lack the strength to do the back-breaking work in the fields. The summer corn and rye look stunted, and I haven't seen any wheat at all.

Charles watched two scrawny and weak-looking men dig listlessly in a patch of onion plants. "They're starving!" he exclaimed. "How much longer can France go on like this?"

Charles's stomach rumbled loudly. *That reminds me— I haven't eaten since this morning in Paris.* His mind turned to dinner at the château. The food would be excellent, as always, but he would be dining with his uncle, the marquis. Charles's stomach immediately stopped rumbling.

The coach climbed slowly to the top of a steep hill and then stopped. Charles pushed open the coach door with his nose and hopped out to gaze upon the Evrémonde lands.

At the bottom of the hill, the tiny village sat at the edge of a sweeping valley that ended in another steep rise. Charles's sharp eyes could make out the church tower in the distance, the windmill, and the forest where the marquis hunted. A stone fortress that was used as a prison sat on top of a hill. The château remained out of sight.

I did have some happy times as a pup when I roamed these lands by myself. I got to know the people, the fields, the streams, every tree. . . .

He sighed and then hopped back easily into the coach. A moment later, it skidded down the hill and came to a stop next to the old fountain in the village square. Charles knew the village, too. He recognized the tannery, tavern, stable yard, brewery, and a dozen or so houses, all small and in bad condition, grouped around the square. He glanced at the posting house, where coaches would exchange tired horses for a fresh team.

Several people sat in doorways, peeling onions and scraping potatoes as they prepared their humble suppers. One elderly woman, bent over her crude wood cane, hobbled out of her cottage. Charles could smell misery in the heavy air. He could also feel the eyes of every villager watching the coach.

"Monsieur!" a voice called out. "Monsieur Charles!"

Charles's ears pricked up. He recognized the voice. He leaned his head out the window. He saw a heavy-set man with a fringe of gray hair around his otherwise bald head hurrying toward the coach. He was waving his tricorne—a triangular-shaped hat—and breathing heavily.

"Monsieur Gabelle!" Charles said with pleasure. His tail wagged as he stretched out a paw in greeting. He liked this man who ran the posting house and collected taxes for the marquis. Charles knew he was a good-hearted man who could be trusted.

Monsieur Gabelle grasped Charles's paw and bowed slightly. "Ah, Monsieur Charles, it's good to see you again. It's been so long—five years, I think. I had heard that when you left France, you moved to London. Are you living there now?"

Charles nodded.

"I'm sure you've seen we're not doing well in France," Monsieur Gabelle continued in a lowered voice. "I know you're on your way to the château, but I wanted to inform you of something quite strange that just happened."

"Something strange?" Charles asked.

Monsieur Gabelle's eyes darted around the square. He leaned close to Charles's ear and lowered his voice even more. "Spies everywhere, you know." Then he whispered, "Just an hour ago, the marquis's carriage came by—over the hill and through the village."

Charles nodded. "My uncle has just returned from Paris."

Monsieur Gabelle continued. "One of the local fellows happened to be walking nearby when the marquis's carriage stopped at the top of the hill. This fellow claims he saw a tall, thin man completely covered with dust riding *underneath* the carriage."

"*Underneath* the carriage?" Charles asked.

"Yes!" Gabelle whispered. "The man was stretched out like a corpse and hanging onto the carriage chain. When the carriage stopped, the man jumped off, rolled down the side of the hill, then disappeared. He must have hidden in the underbrush."

"A tall, thin man?"

"Precisely," Gabelle answered. "A tall, thin man covered with dust from head to toe—like a ghost!"

"Does my uncle know about this?" Charles asked.

Gabelle shook his head. "The fellow who saw it was afraid to tell anyone until after the marquis had left the village."

Charles thought for a moment and then held out his paw again. "Thank you for the information, Monsieur Gabelle. I'd better hurry to the château now. My uncle does not like to be kept waiting."

Gabelle pressed the paw in his hand. "*Au revoir*—good-bye, Monsieur Charles."

The coach jolted forward. Charles slipped back into the deep shadows of the interior. His dark eyes stared straight ahead. For several minutes, he thought of nothing but two terrible images: first, a tall, thin man in the Saint Antoine district in Paris holding the limp body of a dead child; and second, a tall, thin, dust-covered man hanging onto the underside of the marquis's carriage.

Charles became aware of a new sound. The wheels of the coach were no longer rolling over hard ground. He recognized the crunching and scraping of wheels on gravel. He quickly looked out of the carriage. The fur on his head and neck bristled.

"The Château Saint Evrémonde!" he murmured.

The sight of his ancestors' home never failed to chill Charles to the bone. He felt a mixture of awe and disgust. As the coach slowed and then stopped, Charles gazed up at the massive building, constructed two hundred years earlier, in the late 1500s.

Three tall stories of carved stone blocks, stone balconies, and stone railings rose to meet the steep slate roof. Dozens of small panes of dark glass were set into each stone window frame. A pair of sweeping stone stairways curved toward each other and joined to form a wide terrace in front of the

huge front door. Carved heads of lions alternating with carved heads of humans decorated the railings. At each of the four corners of the château, a tall, round tower stood guard over the Evrémonde estate.

"Home, sweet home," Charles muttered.

"Monsieur Charles?"

Startled, Charles glanced down and saw one of the marquis's servants approach the coach with a torch. The natural light had faded, and the first stars were already twinkling in the sky. The servant bowed as he opened the coach door and lowered the steps. Charles scampered down to the ground, while another servant took his traveling bag.

Charles trotted toward the château alongside the servant who held the torch. He breathed in the aroma of stately plane trees, poplars, and pines. As they mounted one of the grand staircases, the front door swung open. A third servant stepped outside with another torch. He bowed as Charles passed through the entrance. Yet another servant appeared and took Charles's lightweight coat.

"The marquis would inform you that dinner awaits. The marquis wishes for you to come to the table now," the servant said.

"Certainly," Charles replied.

Charles crossed the immense hall behind the servant. His paws moved lightly on the uncarpeted stone floor, but the clicking sound of his nails produced an echo. The servants had closed off the adjoining reception rooms for the night. Charles observed that nothing had changed during his five-year absence. A collection of boar spears, swords, hunting knives, and riding whips comprised the decoration of the grim hall. *This is my uncle's idea of a warm welcome,* he thought.

Charles and the servant climbed a wide staircase and entered the long corridor that led to the marquis's private apartment. At the end of the corridor, the servant opened a heavy oak door and bowed as Charles stepped through the doorway.

His scent! Charles's eyes closed for an instant. *I'd recognize that scent anywhere in the world! The splendor, the cruelty, the Evrémonde history!* Charles's face quivered.

"Monsieur?" the servant murmured.

Charles shook himself and trotted briskly across the reception room. Like the rest of the marquis's apartment, it was furnished in a combination of styles: delicate gilded and painted pieces from the period of King Louis XIV; and much older, heavier furniture that had been in the family for centuries.

Charles entered the room where the marquis ate his meals when he dined alone. It was a round room with a high, vaulted ceiling, located in one of the château's four towers. The servants had opened the single large window to the summer air, but they had closed the wooden blinds.

Charles's eyes focused on the marquis, who sat at the dinner table with his back to the door. The nobleman slowly pushed back his chair, stood, and nodded to Charles in his most courtly manner. His expression remained calm, but he did not offer his hand, and Charles did not offer his paw. The marquis motioned for Charles to sit in the chair on the opposite side of the table, where a place was set.

Charles jumped gracefully onto his seat. He picked up his folded napkin with his teeth, shook it open, and tucked it neatly into his white-linen neck band.

"It's taken you quite a long time to get here," the marquis said.

"On the contrary," Charles replied. "I made very good time, considering the distance from London."

"I mean," the marquis said, "that it has taken you five years to decide to make this trip." A faint smile played around his thin, pale lips.

Charles's whiskers quivered. "I've been delayed by . . ."—he hesitated, then added lamely—". . . business."

"No doubt," the marquis answered in his polished voice.

Charles looked down at the table as a servant placed a porcelain plate filled with soup in front of him. He sniffed the delicious-smelling steam. *Oyster bisque made with the finest Cognac,* he thought. His tongue darted out to sample the soup. He felt a queasy tremor in his empty belly and sighed. *I can't eat with my uncle. He isn't fit company for a cat!*

Charles shook his head. "I'm afraid, *monsieur,* that my stomach is unsettled after my journey. I can't eat anything— except perhaps a biscuit."

"I'm sorry for your inconvenience," the marquis said with perfect politeness. He raised his soup spoon to his lips.

Charles and the marquis did not exchange another word while the marquis finished his dinner and the servants remained in the room, always attentive toward their master and his needs.

This is slow torture, Charles thought, *like having dinner in the Bastille prison in Paris with the executioner!*

"What is that?" the marquis asked, breaking the long silence. "That noise outside the window." He looked directly at Charles. "You always had such keen ears. Did you hear that?"

"I'm afraid not," Charles said. "My mind was elsewhere." He turned around on his chair to face the window.

The marquis gestured to a servant. "Open the blinds."

The servant threw the blinds wide open and leaned out the window. Soon after, he turned to the marquis. "*Monseigneur,* there's nothing outside but the trees and the night."

"Good," the marquis said. "Close the blinds."

When the marquis had finished eating, the servants cleared the table, served the coffee, then withdrew from the room. Charles sprang from his chair and walked over to the fireplace. He turned to face his uncle.

"You know why I've come," Charles said.

"I do?" the marquis murmured.

"You know," Charles continued, "that in the last moments of her life, my dear mother made one request. She begged me to make up for all the crimes committed by my father—your older brother—when he was marquis—"

"Your father committed no crimes," the marquis interrupted. "And I, the heir to the title when he died, have also committed no crimes."

Charles returned to his seat at the table, placed his front paws on the white-brocade cloth, and leaned toward the marquis. "Our family has abused our power and position for centuries. We have behaved so terribly for so long that 'Evrémonde' is the most hated name in France!"

"I should hope so," the marquis responded. He crossed his silk-clad legs. "Hatred is the respect that the low-born people automatically pay to the high-born of society." He shook the ruffled cuffs of his shirt gently and reached into a lace-trimmed pocket for his tobacco box. "Fear and slavery, my friend, are necessary to keep the low-born human beasts obedient to the whip. I will preserve the honor of our family, even if you will not."

Charles raised his voice in anger. "Our family honor means as much to me as it does to you. But I will defend it by cleansing the Evrémonde name. When you die, the estate will pass to me. I will become the marquis. I plan to give up my title. I will give the land to the peasants who have been slaves on it. I will do my best to see that the next generation working on this land has a better life."

The marquis gave Charles a grim smile. "And I will die upholding the system under which I have lived." The marquis uncrossed his legs and stood up. "You must be tired, Monsieur Charles. Shall we end our conversation for tonight?"

Charles hopped down from his chair. He could feel his four legs trembling with anger. "Just a moment more."

The marquis smiled. "An hour more, if you so choose."

Charles took a few tense steps up and down the length of the room. His nails tapped sharply on the floor. "I know you will try to prevent me from ever claiming this estate as mine. You will destroy me, if necessary. You already have your spies working in England."

The marquis sighed. "I find this kind of conversation needlessly unpleasant. But I do have a final question for you. How do you plan to live once you have given away your property?"

Charles glared at his uncle. "For many generations, Evrémondes have been too lazy to work at anything. But I have worked like a dog to earn a living in London. And I will continue to do so."

"An Evrémonde who works," the marquis murmured. "How charming. You're doing a fine job of upholding the family name." He reached for the small silver bell on the table and rang it.

Charles's tail thumped impatiently. "I'm sure your spies have told you that I changed my name. In England, I am called Charles Darnay."

A servant entered the room.

"Show *monsieur,* my nephew, to his bedchamber," the marquis said. His pale face was as calm and motionless as a mask.

Charles turned away from his uncle and thought, *The order you'd really like to give your servants is: "Burn monsieur, my nephew, in his bed!"*

Charles walked wearily down the corridor by the light of the servant's torch. In his room, he pulled off his clothes by the light of a candle whose flame never flickered in the still summer air. He jumped from a low stool onto the high

29

mattress and then pulled the gauze bed curtains closed with his teeth. The silk sheets felt wonderfully cool against his fur. He soon fell into a deep sleep.

AAAAAHHHH!

Charles awoke to the sound of a dreadful scream. A moment later, he heard shouting, which seemed to come from the far end of the corridor. He leaped from his bed to the floor, seized his dressing gown in his teeth, and flung it over his shoulders. Footsteps drummed on the stone floor outside his room. He pulled open his door and bounded into the corridor.

The marquis's valet ran out of his master's private apartment shrieking. Charles's fur stood on end, and his heart pounded as he raced toward the reception room. In the middle of the room, a butler bent over the slumped figure of a young footman who had fainted. A half-dozen other servants were rushing into the round room where the marquis had dined the night before.

Charles squeezed between their tangled legs and glanced around the dining room, his tongue hanging out, panting. He bolted through the open door to the marquis's bedchamber. Through the half-open blinds, a shaft of early morning light pierced the room. More servants leaned over the marquis's enormous bed, but they moved back the instant they saw Charles. With one great vault, he was up on the bed.

The marquis lay perfectly still, his head resting on a satin pillow. His skin was as smooth and pale as always, but his face no longer carried its carefully controlled expression. Instead, his features looked horribly angry. Charles leaned forward.

A knife had been driven deep into the marquis's heart. A piece of paper fluttered around the handle of the weapon. Charles read the words scrawled on the paper:

Send Evrémonde straight to his tomb!
This—from the people of Saint Antoine!

Murder! My paws still tremble when I think of it. With one rapid thrust of a knife, the world of the Evrémondes changed forever. The title of "marquis" passed to Charles. . . .

Back in Oakdale, however, nothing is changing. Joe and David can't solve the baby-sitting problem. They are stuck in the same place. Meanwhile, my paws are itching to be on the move.

Chapter Four

Wishbone perched on an armchair in the living room, his body tense, his eyes darting between David and Joe. David rolled his remote-control car back and forth along the back of the couch. Joe leaned against the kitchen doorjamb, one foot tapping the floor. Emily and Tina sat on the couch with their arms crossed and their lips pursed.

Wishbone thumped his tail. "Okay, people, let's make a decision. We're losing valuable play time here. You know the pup's saying—waste not time, want not fun."

Joe sighed. "Why don't the girls stay inside while we go outside to test the car?"

"Yes!" Emily cheered.

David hesitated for an instant. He pointed a finger at his sister. "Emily, this is Joe's house. I don't want you to touch anything or mess anything up." He gave her a stern look. "Do you understand?"

Emily and Tina smiled at each other and nodded at David.

Wishbone grunted. "Why am I not convinced?"

Joe headed for the front door. "Let's go."

David followed, carrying the car and the remote-control unit. "You guys be good!" he called over his shoulder when he reached the door.

Wishbone looked at the girls and flexed his shoulders. *This is where the dog exits—fast!* He jumped down from the chair. "Excuse me, ladies, but I must leave you now."

Wishbone turned toward the hallway. Emily pounced on him and grabbed his leather collar. "We get Wishbone!" she declared.

"Yes!" Tina chimed in. She leaned over and clasped her arms around Wishbone's belly.

Wishbone strained to get away. His front legs thrashed in the air, but it was no use. "It's two against one. That's not fair. I demand justice!"

"Let's make Wishbone pretty," Emily suggested.

Wishbone glared at her. "Excuse me, but I am not a poodle. I do not wish to be 'pretty.'"

Tina nodded. "Let's put a bow on him."

Wishbone gagged. "First I lose my freedom. Next goes my dignity."

Emily let go of Wishbone's collar. Then she began to search inside her backpack, which was lying on the couch. "I have a big bow in here."

Tina reached toward the backpack and began to help Emily search.

Wishbone quickly stretched out his front legs and crept forward. He kept his eyes on the front door, which was open a few inches. *If I can just get through that door,* he thought, *I'm out of here!* He reached the hallway, stood up, and pushed the door open with his nose. He looked back at the girls. "See ya—ha!"

With a single leap, Wishbone cleared the front steps and sprinted across the lawn.

"Born to be free! Yes! I love being a dog!" He headed for the sidewalk, where he saw Joe and David testing the remote-control car. "Boy's best friend will now complete the happy scene."

Wishbone came to a halt at Joe's right leg. *I'm finally back where I belong,* he thought, *with people I can trust.*

"Hi, guys," someone called out.

Wishbone, Joe, and David turned their heads in the direction of the house next door to Joe's. Its owner, Wanda Gilmore, was working on the engine of her car, which was parked in her driveway. Wanda waved the greasy rag she held in her hand and started to walk toward Wishbone and the boys. She looked as lively as usual in her yellow-print blouse and loose jacket with the plaid collar and cuffs. Her maroon hat covered her short, dark hair, except for the bangs, which reached the top of her eyebrows.

"Wishbone," Joe said, "check this out."

Joe pressed the Start button on the remote-control unit and sent the car racing down the sidewalk. Pressing another button, he made the car turn right and speed up his driveway.

Wishbone began to bark. "I like it! I love it! I want it!" His tail wagged wildly.

"This is amazing, David," Wanda said.

"Thanks, Miss Gilmore," David replied.

"Do you guys think I could give it a try?" Wanda asked.

Joe and David exchanged worried glances.

"Uh . . . sure," David said politely.

Joe handed Wanda the remote unit. She took it with one hand. With her other hand, she gave Joe her greasy rag.

"Not a great trade, Joe," Wishbone muttered.

Wanda stared down at the remote unit. Her eyes gleamed, and she smiled. "I like living life in the fast lane." She raised her arm until the remote was straight out in front of her. "Gentlemen, start your engines!"

She pressed a button. The little car whipped around in a circle and zoomed up the driveway.

Wishbone barked once and took off at top speed. "I really want that car. I've got to have it!"

Wanda thrust out her lower lip and blew hard. "Vr-r-r-o-o-o-m-m! Vr-r-r-o-o-o-m-m! Vr-r-r-o-o-o-m-m-m!"

Joe and David laughed. Wanda made the car loop across the lawn and back toward the sidewalk. Wishbone charged after it.

"This is thrilling!" Wanda exclaimed.

Wishbone dodged in front of the car and then scampered behind it. He darted back and forth as it changed directions. He ran alongside it. "Hey, you! Pull over! Let me see some I.D., pal."

Wanda's eyes flicked back and forth—from the remote unit to the car to Wishbone. She pressed a button, and the car turned onto her own lawn. Wishbone barked and dashed across its path. Wanda pressed two other buttons at the same time. The car turned and began speeding toward Wishbone.

"David!" Wanda screamed. "How do you stop this thing?"

"Wishbone, get out of the way!" Joe shouted.

35

David grabbed the remote unit. The car swerved away from Wishbone. It headed for a huge tree. David groped frantically for the Off switch. Just as he found it—

Crash!

"Oh, man!" David moaned.

Wanda ran to the tree. David and Joe rushed after her. Wishbone got there first.

The car had spun over on its side. Its wheels had stopped turning. Wishbone sniffed it. "Oops! Let me just say that I didn't do it."

David, Joe, and Wanda bent over the car. David picked it up carefully and examined it. The antenna jiggled too loosely, the front bumper was bent, and one wheel fell off in David's hand.

"Oh, David, I'm so sorry," Wanda said. "Wishbone got in the way, and I panicked."

David turned the car over. "That's okay, Miss Gilmore," he said in a low voice.

"Joe," Wanda said, "you should keep Wishbone away from this thing."

Wishbone's ears stood up. His jaw dropped open. "What? She's the one who doesn't know how to drive!"

Joe bent down toward Wishbone. "Sorry, but I just don't want you to get hurt."

Wishbone took a cautious step back. "Okay, so keep her off the road, and I'll be fine."

Joe grasped Wishbone's collar.

Not again! Wishbone thought. *Getting collared like this is getting old fast.*

Joe pulled Wishbone toward their house.

Wishbone looked at where he was going with horror. He dragged his hind legs. "No, no! Joe, you don't understand—that's a Danger Zone. Believe me—you don't want to be responsible for what might happen to me in there!"

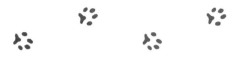

I'm getting dragged into a Danger Zone, and there's nothing I can do about it.

Something similar has happened to Charles Darnay. He leaves France immediately after his uncle's murder, thinking he is getting himself *out* of a Danger Zone. He hopes to return to a life of peace and quiet in London, England. But then—like me—he suddenly finds himself dragged into more danger than he has ever known.

Chapter Five

One month had passed since Charles Darnay had gazed upon the body of his murdered uncle. Now he stood outside the double doors of the courtroom in London's famous criminal court called the Old Bailey. The strong legs of two prison guards pressed against his sides. Charles shook his head as if he still wasn't able to believe where he had ended up.

One moment, I'm traveling on the ferry from France to England, truly content. I had made arrangements for the peasants on the Evrémonde lands to be treated kindly, and not be taxed at all. The next moment, I step off the ferry and I'm arrested by the English authorities as a foreign spy!

The courtroom doors swung open. Charles's glance quickly took in the judge's bench and the witness box. The witness box was a small platform enclosed by wood railings where witnesses stood to answer questions asked by lawyers. He saw the larger jury box where the jurors sat, the tables where the lawyers shuffled piles of papers, and, finally, a small platform called the dock.

That's where the prisoner on trial stands. A shudder rippled through the fur on Charles's shoulders. *That's me!* He gritted his teeth, thinking for the thousandth time how his uncle, the marquis, must have planned to have him arrested in England as a foreign spy. "His last good deed before going to heaven," Charles muttered bitterly.

"Come on, you!" the sentry at the door growled.

Squeezed between the guards to his right and left, Charles walked into the courtroom with his sleek white-and-brown furred head held high. He stepped up to the platform of the dock and placed his front paws carefully on the wood slab at the front. The court clerks had scattered herbs on the slab, and on every other horizontal surface in the room. Charles's soft black nose twitched.

Herbs and vinegar are sprinkled everywhere. It's supposed to ward off the jail fever that prisoners carry in from the filthy English jails. Charles gave himself a discreet scratch with a hind leg. *They should find something to keep away fleas, too.*

Chattering Londoners crammed into the courtroom's visitors' balcony by the dozens. They had each paid several pennies to see the afternoon trial. Charles watched them as they pressed forward and rocked from side to side, straining to get a good look at him. His sharp ears picked up snatches of conversation.

"What's he on trial for?"

"Treason. They say he's a spy for France."

"That'll be a good show. They'll hang him for sure and then cut him into quarters."

"Too bad, eh? He's a nice-looking fellow in one piece."

Charles stopped listening. He stared down at his front paws and willed them to be still—so still that they didn't stir a single herb on the slab of wood.

My uncle must have planned this trap months ago, he thought. *But the charges are so clearly false—I have to believe that justice will win out in the end!*

"Silence in the court!" a guard called out.

The sound of voices chattering in the balcony dropped

to a low buzz. The judge entered the courtroom wearing the traditional English long curled white wig and a long black robe. He took his seat at the bench and gave Charles a piercing look. Charles lowered his head and shoulders in a polite bow. The judge turned to two men sitting at a table. One was plump, not more than thirty years old, with a flushed face and pushy manner. He wore a well-pressed black robe and a short, neat white wig. Charles nodded at this man, who was his lawyer, Mr. Stryver.

The second man at the table didn't bother to look at the judge or anyone else. He lounged in his chair, his head tipped back and his half-open eyes fixed on the ceiling. His dirty wig had slid over one ear, and his torn black robe looked as though he had slept in it for a month. His handsome but sloppily shaven face showed the signs of too little sleep and too much wine.

That's my lawyer's associate, Sydney Carton. Charles's tail twitched nervously. He tried to reassure himself. *He looks like something the cat dragged in, but many people think he's the one with the real brains.*

"The attorney general will now inform the jury of the crime for which the prisoner is being tried," the judge announced.

The attorney general, who also wore a white wig and black robe, rose and faced the jury. He spoke in deep, ringing tones.

"The prisoner before you appears young in years, but do not be fooled. He is experienced in the practice of treason—betraying his country. For some five years, he has committed the most hateful, brutal, spiteful, lowly, and destructive sabotage imaginable. He, a Frenchman, has turned against the most generous, fair, and faithful country—the country that gave him refuge—our England! He has betrayed the most generous, fair, and faithful monarch, our King George!"

Charles listened to the buzz of the crowd grow louder.

The attorney general pointed at him and raised his voice. "That vicious, corrupt, wicked, disloyal, sneaky—"

Charles tapped a paw impatiently on the wood slab.

"That traitor," the attorney general finally said, "stole top-secret military information about His Majesty's land and sea forces in the American colonies. Then he sold the information to spies who work for the French king, Louis. The French king is a friend of the American rebels!"

People sitting in the visitors' balcony produced a loud, collective gasp.

Charles's long whiskers quivered with indignation. *I wouldn't steal information for a spy. I wouldn't even fetch a newspaper for a spy!*

The attorney general cleared his throat and called out, "The witness, Miss Lucie Manette, will now come forward."

A small, slim woman, hardly more than twenty years old, walked from her bench to the witness box. Her hair, a mass of golden curls, framed her delicate features and high forehead like a halo. Her skin looked pale against a deep green linen dress. As she stepped up to the platform, her eyes met Charles's eyes. Hers were clear blue and filled with sympathy. She leaned forward slightly, as if she wanted to let Charles know that she believed in his innocence and honor.

Charles and the young woman stared at each other so intently that all other eyes in the courtroom were drawn to them. Even the rumpled Sydney Carton stopped looking at the ceiling.

Charles's heart had started to beat faster. He heard someone in the balcony whisper, "Is she a witness *for* or *against* the prisoner?"

"Against."

The deep voice of the attorney general drowned out the whispers. "Miss Manette, have you ever before seen the prisoner?"

"Yes, once before," she replied. She spoke English with a French accent.

"Describe for the jury the exact circumstances."

Lucie Manette spoke carefully, never taking her eyes off Charles. "One month ago, my father, a friend, and I boarded the ferry boat that runs between the French city of Calais and the English city of Dover. My father was so ill that I was afraid to take him belowdecks and away from the fresh sea air. But the weather was cold and windy, and I didn't know how to shelter him properly. This most generous gentle-man—"

"Are you referring to the prisoner?" the attorney general interrupted.

"Yes."

"Then call him 'the prisoner.'"

Lucie nodded. Her eyes filled with pain for Charles. "The prisoner offered his help and found a way to make a shelter out of blankets. Then he stayed with my father and me during the crossing to make sure we were all right."

"Was the prisoner ever in the company of any other people?" the attorney general asked.

Lucie nodded again. "He boarded the boat with another Frenchman, but that man departed before the boat sailed."

"Did you see the prisoner and this other Frenchman speak or exchange documents?"

Lucie answered, "I saw them speak briefly, and I saw them look at papers together. But I can't say to whom these papers belonged, or if they were exchanged."

"Can you say for certain that the prisoner did *not* give the papers to the other Frenchman?"

Lucie hesitated. "No, I cannot say that for certain." Her forehead wrinkled. She looked frightened. "He was so kind to my father and me. I only hope I haven't caused him harm by speaking today!"

Charles's heart again beat faster under his white, furred chest. *I can't imagine her harming a single hair on any creature's head—or hide.*

The attorney general spoke coldly to Lucie. "Your only duty in this courtroom is to tell the complete truth. You may step down now." As Lucie returned to her seat, he called out, "The next witness, Mr. Jarvis Lorry, will step forward."

A neatly dressed man of about sixty walked to the witness box. He wore a dignified brown jacket, brown waistcoat, and brown breeches with a spotless white collar and fine brown stockings. An odd little brown wig sat on his head. His manner was serious, but his eyes were both intelligent and kind.

"Are you a longtime employee of Tellson's bank, Mr. Lorry?" the attorney general asked.

"Yes, I am a man of business. I have been at Tellson's for forty years—forty rewarding years, I might add."

"Have you ever before seen the prisoner?"

Mr. Lorry explained that he was the friend who had traveled with Lucie Manette and her father on the ferry a month earlier. He said he had seen the prisoner board the boat at Calais with another Frenchman. He had also seen the prisoner speak to this other Frenchman and look at some papers. He could not, however, say that treason was involved.

"Mr. Lorry, did you see anything to indicate that treason was *not* involved?"

Charles snorted quietly. *Treason—my tail! I was with Monsieur Gabelle, who used to collect taxes on the Evrémonde lands. Right after my uncle's murder, I made him my representative. He accompanied me to the ferry. I was giving him instructions on how to improve the lives of the peasants.*

Mr. Lorry hesitated and then spoke. "No, I cannot say for certain that treason was not involved."

"You may step down, Mr. Lorry," the attorney general said. "The next witness is Dr. Alexandre Manette."

A tall gentleman sitting next to Lucie Manette rose. She stood, too, and held on to his arm as if she were afraid to let him go. He patted her hand gently, smiled to reassure her, then walked to the witness box. His energetic pace and alert face showed him to be no more than about fifty years old. But his hair had already turned snow-white.

"Dr. Manette, when did you first leave France and arrive in England?" the attorney general asked.

"One month ago."

"Did you travel aboard the ferry with Miss Manette and Mr. Jarvis Lorry? The jury requires your version of the events that the previous witnesses have described."

"I'm sorry, but I have no memory of that voyage."

"Will you explain why?" the attorney general asked.

Dr. Manette suddenly looked confused and hesitant. He raised a hand to his eyes, then let it drop.

"Was it because you had just been released from

44

prison?" the attorney general continued. "Isn't it true that you were secretly imprisoned without trial in your native land? Didn't you spend eighteen years in the Bastille in Paris?"

The crowd gasped. Dr. Manette didn't seem to notice anything. He stood slightly stooped, his forehead creased, his eyes vacant. In the course of a minute, he appeared to have aged thirty years. Lucie rose to her feet, her face filled with pain. She reached a hand out toward her father.

Charles's paw angrily brushed away the herbs lying on the wood slab in front of him. He remembered catching sight of the Bastille prison in Paris the day before his uncle's murder. *Eighteen years in the Bastille! An aristocrat must have ordered the doctor to be imprisoned without a trial. How did the poor man survive such an ordeal?*

A voice interrupted Charles's restless thoughts.

"Officer! Help that young lady! Can't you see she's about to faint?"

Sydney Carton had spoken. Somehow, even while staring at the ceiling, he alone had noticed Lucie sway dizzily. A low moan escaped from Charles's lips as he watched a guard escort Lucie to the door. She kept her eyes fixed on her father the entire time. The murmur of the crowd grew louder. The judge motioned for another guard to help Dr. Manette step out of the witness box and move toward the door.

Over the hubbub from the balcony, the attorney general called out, "The witness John Barsad will now step forward."

"Quiet in the court!" the judge commanded.

Charles's head snapped around so quickly to look at the witness that his ears flapped. *John Barsad—that sponge who used to hang around me! What is he doing here?*

A gentleman in his mid-thirties, dressed in a well-cut but worn black coat and breeches, stepped up to the witness box. He had black hair, cool gray eyes, and an unpleasant manner. The attorney general led him carefully through his testimony point by point.

Yes, he, John Barsad, had once been a close friend of the prisoner. Yes, he had begun to suspect several years ago that the prisoner was a spy for the French. Yes, he had urged the prisoner's servant to search the prisoner's personal belongings for evidence. Yes, the servant had found lists of His Majesty's troop positions in the American colonies hidden among the prisoner's clothing. Yes, the servant had given him, John Barsad, the lists. Yes, he, John Barsad, had turned the lists over to His Majesty's Chief Secretary of State.

The attorney general took a pile of wrinkled papers from a table and held them high for the jury and John Barsad to see. "Do you recognize these papers, Mr. Barsad?"

"Yes. They are the very lists of His Majesty's troop positions that were found among the prisoner's belongings."

Another buzz rose from the visitors' balcony. Again, Charles picked up snatches of conversation there.

"He sold our soldiers down the river, did he? The scoundrel!"

"Those papers will cause him to hang for sure, and I'm glad of it!"

The attorney general asked Mr. Barsad a final question. "Why did you take the personal risk of having the prisoner's belongings searched?"

"Because," John Barsad replied, "I am a loyal subject of His Majesty King George."

A low growl rumbled in Charles's throat. *Loyal subject! Then I'm the local dog catcher!*

The attorney general nodded at Barsad. "You have done your country a superb service. You are certainly one of the great patriots of English history!"

The buzz from the balcony rose to a high pitch. The crowd leaned forward to see Charles's reaction.

They're like frenzied flies swarming around dead meat! Charles thought. *Only they're buzzing around* me!

Barsad started to step down from the witness box.

The attorney general began, "Will the next witness—"

No! Charles looked at his lawyers across the room. *Do something! Stop this charade! You know everything Barsad says is a lie! You've got to cross-examine him!*

Charles felt a terrible pressure around his throat. He tried to loosen his collar. He touched the fur beneath it. *I can't breathe! They're putting a noose around my neck!*

Chapter Six

Charles continued to glare at his lawyers, but they didn't seem to notice. Sydney Carton stopped looking at the ceiling long enough to scribble a few words on a piece of paper. He crumpled the paper into a ball and tossed it to Mr. Stryver. Mr. Stryver glanced at the paper and stood up.

"Mr. Attorney General, my colleague, Mr. Sydney Carton, would like to ask a few questions of the witness, John Barsad."

It's about time! Charles thought with great relief.

The attorney general looked annoyed, but he nodded his head at Sydney Carton, who was busy once more staring at the ceiling. Mr. Carton pushed his soiled wig from one side of his head to the other and stood up lazily. He shrugged his shoulders and, with no introduction, began firing a steady stream of questions at the witness.

"What is your profession, Mr. Barsad?" Sydney Carton asked.

"I'm a gentleman," replied Barsad.

"What income do you live on, Mr. Barsad?"

"Income from . . . my land."

"Where is your land, Mr. Barsad?"

"I . . . I can't recall right now—not that it's anyone's business."

"Have you ever been in prison, Mr. Barsad?"

"Never."

"You've never been in debtors' prison, Mr. Barsad?"

"Maybe once or twice."

"Just once or twice, Mr. Barsad?"

"Well . . . maybe five or six times."

"Have you ever been kicked down stairs for cheating at dice, Mr. Barsad?"

"Maybe."

"Who kicked you down the stairs for cheating, Mr. Barsad?"

Barsad snarled at Sydney Carton, "You did."

"Mr. Barsad, isn't it true that you make your living by gambling?"

"Not any more than other gentlemen do."

"Did you ever borrow any money from the prisoner, Mr. Barsad?"

"Yes."

"Did you pay him back, Mr. Barsad?"

"No."

"Isn't it true that you were only an acquaintance of the prisoner's, not a good friend, Mr. Barsad?"

"That's not my opinion."

"Isn't the servant who found the lists in the prisoner's belongings an old friend of yours, Mr. Barsad?"

"Yes—so what?"

"Didn't you take those lists yourself and have the servant plant them in the prisoner's belongings, Mr. Barsad?"

John Barsad turned white with anger. "No!"

Sydney Carton kept up his rapid-fire assault. "Didn't someone pay you to set this trap for the prisoner, Mr. Barsad?"

"No!"

"Aren't *you* the spy in this case, Mr. Barsad?"

"No!"

"Aren't you a longtime gambler, cheat, and liar, Mr. Barsad?"

The noise from the gallery drowned out the witness's last answer. As comments from the crowd flew back and forth, Charles pricked up his ears to hear them.

"How'd you like this last witness? A scoundrel or not?"

"He's no saint."

"We might not get that hanging, after all. Too bad—it's been at least a week since we've had a good hanging."

Sydney Carton yawned, sat down in his chair, and pulled his wig over his eyes, looking as if he were going to take a nap.

Charles's tail wagged. *Bravo, Mr. Carton! You destroyed Barsad as a witness! Chewed him up and spat him out just like an old shoe!*

The judge demanded quiet in the courtroom, but a low hum continued to come from the visitors' balcony. The attorney general called Charles's servant to the witness box. Imitating Sydney Carton's method, Mr. Stryver showed the servant to be a liar and betrayer.

The jury left the courtroom to decide on its verdict. All the people in the visitors' balcony went outside to drink ale and eat the meat pies on sale in the courtyard. Charles moved to the back of the dock. He hopped onto the bench there and sat down. He calmed himself. Only the clicking sound of his nails as he tapped one of his paws on the wood revealed nervousness.

Charles's thoughts turned to Lucie Manette. *I pray she's all right. How kind her eyes are. How sensitive. How generous. How blue. How—*

"I suppose you're thinking about Miss Manette."

Startled, Charles whirled around. Sydney Carton

leaned against the railing of the dock. He was examining his own very dirty fingernails.

"How is she?" Charles asked. "Has she recovered? How is Dr. Manette?"

"They're both much better," Sydney Carton replied. "In fact, they're well enough to return to the courtroom for the end of this show."

"Could you tell them for me that I'm so relieved to hear they're better?" Charles asked.

Carton shrugged. "I *could* tell them that. I suppose I will, if you ask me."

Charles's mouth dropped open slightly. "Well, of course—I *am* asking you. Will you be so kind as to pass on the message?"

Carton nodded absentmindedly. "By the way, what do you think the verdict will be?"

Charles sighed and rubbed his forehead with his paw. "I'm hoping for the best—but preparing myself for the worst."

Carton scratched his chin. "It's always best to prepare for the worst in life." He half-smiled and wandered out the courtroom door.

What a strange fellow he is, Charles thought.

His ears picked up the muffled sound of voices and footsteps. Moments later, the courtroom doors swung open. The jury filed in, followed close behind by the crowd from the visitors' balcony. A moment more, and all the participants and observers had taken their former places.

Charles's heart was beating so hard and so fast that he believed everyone in the room could hear and see it. In reality, he held himself so still that only his whiskers and lips trembled slightly. *My life hangs in the balance. I will walk out of here free and whole, or be hanged and thrown into a hole like the dead body of a stray!*

The judge turned to the foreman of the jury. "Has the jury reached a verdict?"

The foreman stood. "Yes, we have."

"What say you all?" the judge asked.

The eyes of the foreman met Charles's steady gaze. "We find the prisoner . . . *not guilty.*"

Charles's eyes closed for a second. He suddenly felt weak. Then a wave of sweet relief swept over him. His furred body shivered. His tail wagged. He turned, looked up, and his eyes met Lucie Manette's clear blue gaze. She smiled at him.

Five minutes later, the Old Bailey court was as empty as a theater after a performance. Charles stood outside the iron gates at the main entrance with Lucie Manette, Dr. Manette, and Jarvis Lorry. The sun had set. The streetlamps were lit.

"I must thank you for the kind words during your testimony," Charles said to Lucie. He took one of her delicate hands in his paw and kissed it with deep feeling. "I hope you will allow me to call on you and your esteemed father."

"Certainly," Lucie replied. "I'm so relieved that the outcome of your ordeal is a happy one. If Mr. Carton were here, I would congratulate him for his outstanding work. Good night, Mr. Darnay."

Charles turned to say good-bye to Dr. Manette. To Charles's surprise, the doctor stared at him with an expression of distrust and dislike. Breathing in sharply, Charles took a step back when the doctor's expression turned into genuine hate.

How awful! Charles thought. *But why? Have I done something wrong?*

The expression of hate shifted next into one of fear, then confusion. The vacant look that had come into the doctor's eyes in the courtroom returned. Again, he raised a hand to his eyes, then let it drop. Again, he seemed to grow much older in only a moment's time.

"Father," Lucie said gently, pressing his arm.

"Your father is tired," Jarvis Lorry said. Patting his odd little wig to make sure it was in place, he took a step toward the curb. "I'll get a carriage right away and escort you home."

Charles had already trotted to the curb. He barked at the first empty carriage so that it stopped. He waited until Lucie, Dr. Manette, and Jarvis Lorry had departed safely.

"Strange night, isn't it?"

At the sound of the unexpected voice, Charles turned. His sharp eyes detected movement in the darkest shadows near the court building.

Sydney Carton stepped out into the lamplight. "It must be strange for you, standing at liberty outside those walls. You could be inside, preparing to meet your end."

"I have you to thank for my life," Charles said. "I feel the deepest gratitude, Mr. Carton."

Carton yawned. He had taken off his wig and robe, but he looked just as untidy as before. Charles sniffed and recognized the smell of port wine.

"I don't want gratitude," Carton said, "and I don't deserve it. First of all, I didn't do so very much. Second, I don't know why I did it. Do you think I like you?"

The fur on Charles's back bristled. "You acted as if you did in the courtroom, but now—"

"Let me ask you one question," Carton interrupted. "Is it worth almost losing your life if a certain pair of blue eyes looks at you with such compassion?"

Charles opened his mouth, but he didn't know what to say.

Carton went right on. "I assure you, Mr. Darnay, such lovely eyes as Lucie Manette's will never look at me with kindness. Life has no good in it for me—except the good of port wine."

Charles felt pity for the unhappy man. "I'm sure—"

Carton interrupted him again. "You can be sure of nothing, except that I am a disappointed, miserable person. I care for no one on earth, and no one cares for me." Carton turned and walked away.

Charles watched the unhappy man disappear into the shadows. He felt exhausted. He ached from head to tail. He stepped into the street to look for a carriage. Not seeing one, he started walking toward his rooming house. Only the thought of meeting Lucie Manette again made him feel eager for the next day. But another thought troubled him.

What could possibly make Dr. Manette dislike me—even hate and fear me? I have only respect and admiration for him. There's some mystery here—a deep secret. I don't know why, but I have an unmistakable feeling that it could shatter both our lives!

Charles Darnay has an unmistakable feeling that trouble is brewing for the future.

Back in Oakdale, I know trouble is brewing in the present, with Emily and Tina alone in the house. The signs are unmistakable, but Joe and David don't want to see them.

Chapter Seven

Joe put Wishbone back in the house and shut the front door behind him. He jogged across the lawn. David was kneeling on the sidewalk. He held the miniature car in one hand and a small screwdriver in the other.

"What's the damage?" Joe asked.

David finished tightening a screw and looked up. "I should be able to fix it. How are my sister and Tina?"

"Oh, they're fine," Joe answered.

He stooped down to see what David was doing. He watched until the sound of a bicycle made them both turn around.

"Hi, Sam," Joe called out, waving to the girl riding toward them.

"Hey, you're just in time," David said.

Samantha Kepler braked next to the boys. She hopped off her bike and held it by the handlebar with one hand. With the other hand, she pushed up the black-and-red baseball cap that covered her blond ponytail. Sam lived just a few blocks away and was best friends with Wishbone, Joe, and David. She was smart, loyal, and good at sports.

"Just in time for what?" she asked.

"To see the remote-control car I built in action," David answered. "We had a little accident, but it'll be ready to go in a minute."

"I'll have to see it later," Sam said. "My dad's waiting to take me shopping for new in-line skates. Where's Wishbone? I bet he'd love the car."

"He's in the house with Emily and her friend Tina," Joe answered. "We're baby-sitting."

Sam looked puzzled.

"This baby-sitting thing isn't too bad," Joe said to David.

"Yeah—we don't bother them, and they don't bother us," David said.

"How can you guys call yourselves baby-sitters if they're inside and you're out here?" Sam asked.

David tapped a small metal bar into place. "Don't worry. We have the situation under control."

Samantha didn't looked convinced. She shook her head as she climbed onto her bike. "Whatever you say. I'll see you guys later." She began pedaling up the block.

"'Bye," Joe said.

"See you," David said. He gave the wheels of the car a quick spin. "Now, let's see if I've fixed this."

"I'll get the remote," Joe said. He ran over to the tree and picked up the remote unit, which was lying on the grass.

Wishbone stood on the couch, his nose pressed to the windowpane facing out onto the lawn. He barked for the tenth time. "Come on, Joe! Look this way. Listen up. I have an unmistakable feeling about this situation. Bad! Disaster looms large—larger than me. Joe—"

"Wi-i-i-shbone. Come here, Wi-i-shbone. . . ."

Wishbone spun around. Emily and Tina were walking

slowly toward him. Emily held up a large bow made out of a dozen loops of colored ribbons.

Okay—time for one of my special escape moves, Wishbone thought.

He looked to the right and left. There was no escape. Emily and Tina stepped closer. Wishbone moved back on the couch as far as he could. He pressed his tail and spine deep into the couch pillows. Emily reached out.

Wishbone cringed. "No! No! Not the bow! Anything but the bow!"

My worst fear is about to come true! The ultimate humiliation! And I face it alone. I have only my inner resources to rely on—though, I must say, I have many inner resources. Charles Darnay has to rely on his inner resources, too. After his trumped-up trial for spying, he must use his talents and his strong will to create the life he wants in London.

Chapter Eight

It was a fine summer day in 1781, exactly one year after Charles Darnay's trial at the Old Bailey court. Charles sat motionless, except for his gently wagging tail, on a street corner in the quiet London neighborhood called Soho. Only a few buildings dotted the pavement. Trees, flowers, and patches of grass remained from the time when the area was only woods and fields. Unlike the rest of London, Soho still had some fresh country air.

Charles gazed at the old-fashioned gray house on the opposite corner, where Lucie Manette and her father, Dr. Manette, lived. Despite the warm afternoon sun, a strong emotion made Charles shiver. The white fur on his back quivered. He took a deep breath.

Ah, Lucie, he thought, *lovely, generous, loyal Lucie. Today my life hangs in the balance once again! Today will certainly decide my happiness, my future, my fulfillment— Ouch! My tail!*

"I beg your pardon, sir!" sputtered an elderly gentleman walking with a cane. "I certainly didn't mean to step on you. But I must say, it's most inconvenient to have you plunked down in the middle of the footpath. This is a public road, you know—not a private sitting room."

"You're quite right, sir," Charles said. He dipped his head in a polite bow and moved out of the way. His eyes turned back to gaze at the Manette house. He sighed.

It's been twelve months since I first came to this house to see Lucie and Dr. Manette. So much has happened since then!

As Charles recalled the previous year, his tail wagged faster. He, Jarvis Lorry of Tellson's bank, Dr. Manette, and Lucie had become frequent companions. They dined together at the Manette house every Sunday. In the warm weather, they sat in the tiny courtyard under the plane tree behind the house. They took drives through the countryside in a rented carriage. Sydney Carton sometimes joined them. They had all grown used to Carton's abrupt manners. They weren't surprised when he spent an entire evening standing alone by a window in the Manette home while the rest of them played cards or chatted. He often looked at no one but Lucie.

Charles thought about his own successes. He had earned a reputation in London as a fine tutor of French literature and language. He made a modest but decent income. He wanted no part of his inheritance from his uncle. The money remained in France, where it supported the people who lived on the Evrémonde lands.

Charles's thoughts returned to Lucie. His tail wagged even faster. His heart thumped in his chest. His body tingled. His ears throbbed.

"*Mon amour!*" he murmured. "My love! My—"

He heard rapid footsteps on the path and swished his tail to one side just in time. Two small boys raced by.

"Enough of this!" Charles said. "I must take the plunge—come what may!" He shook himself all over, as if he had just stepped out of a pool of water, and he trotted across the street. He hurried up the brick path to the front door of the Manette house. He lifted the old brass knocker with his paw. Before letting it drop, he took another deep breath.

What happens from now on depends on the outcome of the next half hour!

Charles let the knocker drop. A moment later, he heard a loud clattering on the staircase inside. Then the door flew open.

"Oh, it's *you,* is it?"

Charles had to tip his head so far back to look at the immense woman in the doorway that his ears flopped back. She had a red face, wild red hair, and massive red hands. She had wrapped a scarf the color of cheddar cheese around her head.

"How do you do, Miss Pross?" Charles asked the Manettes' housekeeper.

"I've been better," Miss Pross answered. "For gracious sakes—I could do without running up and down stairs all day for door-knockers like you. If it's my ladybird you're looking for, she's not in." Miss Pross always called Lucie her "ladybird." She adored Lucie. She had cared for her since Lucie was five years old.

"I've come to see Dr. Manette," Charles said.

"Humph!" Miss Pross snorted once, then led the way inside and up the creaky stairs. "Hundreds of your kind, door-knockers, always coming around, always looking for my ladybird, always a bother."

Hundreds of callers for Lucie? Charles asked himself. His whiskers fluttered nervously as his four sturdy legs climbed the stairs. *That's a bad sign.*

"Well?" Miss Pross demanded as soon as they entered the sitting room.

"Could you ask Dr. Manette if he'll receive me?" Charles asked politely.

"For gracious sakes," Miss Pross muttered. She disappeared into the doctor's consulting room, which also served as the dining room. A few seconds later, she reappeared. "He'll see you as soon as he puts away his books and papers." Without another word, she walked out.

Charles listened to her clatter up the stairs. Dr. Manette rented two floors of the house. Miss Pross and Lucie had their bedrooms on the floor above.

Calm down, Charles told himself.

He walked slowly around the room, his paws making almost no sound on the polished floors. The decor showed Lucie's fine taste and her ability to create a charming home with little money. The fresh colors and cheerful patterns of the curtains and cushions went very well with the simple furniture.

Charles sniffed the flowers Lucie had arranged in several vases. He jumped onto a chair and sniffed the sewing she had left on her worktable. He sniffed the book of poetry that she had left sitting on her desk. The entire room carried Lucie's delicate scent.

A heavenly perfume to this nose! Charles thought. He sniffed again and again and again.

"Charles! Is anything wrong? You can't catch your breath? Or do you smell smoke? Is there a fire somewhere?"

Charles spun around and looked at the consulting-room door. The doctor was standing there. "Dr. Manette! I was just . . . uh . . . sniffing the lovely flowers."

Charles hurried to where the doctor stood and offered him a paw. Dr. Manette shook it warmly.

"Excuse me for interrupting your work, Doctor," Charles began. "But I need to talk to you in private about a matter of great importance to me."

Dr. Manette nodded. "Of course, my friend. I'm always glad to see and speak to you. Let's sit in my consulting room."

Charles walked into the room and hopped onto the chair that the doctor indicated. The room reminded Charles of how much the doctor's life had changed in the previous twelve months. After eighteen dreadful years in the Bastille prison, Dr. Manette had taken up his scientific studies again. He had begun seeing patients once more. He was building his reputation as an excellent physician in his adopted country of England.

Most important to Lucie and to the doctor's friends, he seemed to have recovered from his terrible experience in the Bastille. He no longer slipped into and out of a state of confusion, as he had during Charles's trial. He no longer stood with his head down, unable to speak, his eyes vacant. He no longer seemed to turn into a very old man in a matter of moments. And the look of hatred Charles had seen in the doctor's eyes, outside the courtroom one year ago, no longer reappeared.

"You have my complete attention," Dr. Manette said. He moved his chair across from Charles and sat down.

Charles laid his right paw lightly on the doctor's folded hands. "I understand completely, dear Dr. Manette, that the love between you and Lucie is very special. You and she were separated when she was just a baby. Your reunion on this earth is almost a miracle."

"Ah, so you want to talk about Lucie," the doctor murmured. He did not look directly at Charles.

Charles leaned closer, his moist black nose almost touching the doctor's sleeve. His lips and voice trembled. "Yes. I have loved your daughter since the moment I saw her in the Old Bailey courtroom. My love for her has grown deeper and stronger each day. It is, of course, a different kind of love than the love between father and daughter."

Dr. Manette rubbed his forehead and nodded. He still didn't look directly at Charles. "I've already guessed how you feel, and I trust the strength of your feelings, Charles. Have you spoken to Lucie about this?"

"Not a word," Charles said. "I wanted to speak to you first. I wanted to assure you that I will never come between you and Lucie." He pressed the doctor's hands between his tense paws. "If Lucie does love me, I want to ask for her hand in marriage. But—" Charles raised one of his paws. "I wouldn't take her away from this house. I would join the family you have created here."

Dr. Manette stared straight ahead. His eyes were both serious and sad. "The idea of sharing Lucie's love is difficult for me, but it is a good thing. She must live a complete life. She must love someone other than her father." The doctor finally looked right at Charles. "I know you are a fine individual. You have a strong spirit, Charles, and a gentle mind. If Lucie tells me that she loves you, I will consent to your marriage. I promise you this."

A wave of relief passed over Charles like a refreshing breeze across his fur. "Thank you, Dr. Manette! And now, just one last thing. As you already know, 'Darnay' is not my real name. I gave up my name for my own safety, and in order to build a new life in England. But I want to be completely honest with you. I want you to know my real—"

Dr. Manette sprang up from his chair. "No!" he exclaimed.

"Don't tell me! You must not!" He threw up his hands and covered his ears. He took a few nervous steps and then bent down near Charles. He clasped his hands around Charles's muzzle. "Don't say another word about it. I beg you not to!"

Charles couldn't open his mouth. He didn't know whether to nod yes or shake his head no. Dr. Manette squeezed harder.

"If Lucie does love you and wants to be your wife," the doctor said, "tell me your real name the morning of your marriage. But you must never tell Lucie your name! Do you promise?"

Charles nodded as much as he could with his muzzle imprisoned between Dr. Manette's hands. The doctor let his hands drop. He was shaking. Charles was, too.

The doctor made an effort to smile. "And now, my dear friend, I must get back to work. I thank you for speaking to me about this before speaking to Lucie." He grasped Charles's paw and shook it.

Charles knew the doctor was trying to be calm and cheerful. But what he saw in the doctor's eyes made Charles's heart skip a beat. He saw traces of the same distrust and fear that he had seen in the doctor's eyes outside the Old Bailey.

Charles jumped down from his chair and murmured, "Good day, my dear doctor." He turned and walked quickly out of the consulting room and through the sitting room. His nails now made a rapid clicking noise on the floor, but Charles didn't notice.

What upset the doctor so terribly? Charles asked himself. *Why couldn't he bear the idea of hearing my name? I'm positive he doesn't know that my real name is "Evrémonde." Not one person in England knows. So exactly what is this mystery? What is this dreadful secret?*

Charles didn't turn back. He left the house without seeing the frightening change that overcame Dr. Manette.

65

With his head bent down, the doctor shuffled into a corner of the consulting room. He stood there, stooped and silent. One hand gripped his forehead. The other hung limp at his side. His eyes looked empty. He saw nothing. He had turned into a very old man.

Chapter Nine

Exactly six weeks later, a coach stopped in front of the old-fashioned gray house on the quiet corner in Soho.

"We're home!" Lucie exclaimed. She turned to Charles Darnay, who sat beside her in the coach. "My darling husband—we've had such a lovely wedding trip." She rubbed the underside of Charles's muzzle. "While we were away, I didn't think I could ever be happier. But now I see that I am! Now we begin our life together in this dear house, with my beloved father at our side. Nothing could be more perfect!"

She leaned over and kissed the fur on Charles's forehead between his ears. Charles nuzzled her cheek.

Lucie laughed. "Charles! You know that tickles!" She opened the coach door and hopped out before he could help her down.

Charles watched her run to the door of the house and slip inside. He jumped from the coach seat to the cobblestone pavement. The driver quickly carried their bags up the brick path and left them inside the door. Charles pulled his leather coin purse out of his waistcoat pocket with his teeth and paid the man.

"Thank you, and best of luck to you and your bride," the driver said.

Charles walked up to the house with slow, thoughtful steps.

What an amazing six weeks this has been! First I spoke with Dr. Manette about my feelings for Lucie. The next day, I confessed my love to her directly. What happiness! I discovered she felt the same tenderness for me. Just two weeks ago, we were married and then left on our wedding trip.

Charles couldn't hold back a little jump for joy before entering the house. Then he went inside and bounded up the stairs. At the landing, he paused to catch his breath, panting, his tongue hanging out, tail wagging. He calmed himself and thought about Dr. Manette.

I hope he's all right! After my first conversation with him about my feelings for Lucie, he remained in his consulting room, confused and silent for several hours. Lucie described this to me. Then he recovered and was as energetic, busy, and affectionate as ever. But the morning of our marriage . . .

Charles's tail stopped wagging as he went over the scene in his mind. *Dr. Manette looked strained and pale that entire morning. He grew even more tense when the two of us went into his consulting room to talk just before Lucie and I departed for our wedding trip. I told him my real name. It was as if I had struck him with a terrible physical blow. He staggered back and clutched the table. Lucie knocked on the door to say we must leave. The doctor seemed to pull himself together. He had already said his farewell to Lucie, and he insisted that I join her immediately. I left—*

The door to the sitting room swung open. "Ah, there you are!" Dr. Manette exclaimed. "My fine son-in-law! Welcome home!"

The doctor took Charles's paw with one hand and patted him fondly on the shoulder with the other. Charles quickly studied the doctor's face. He looked relaxed, strong, and content. His eyes showed none of the fear or distrust that Charles had noticed before. Charles breathed a deep sigh of relief and stepped into the sitting room.

Miss Pross, Jarvis Lorry, and Sydney Carton had gathered to greet the newlyweds. Miss Pross was already hovering and fussing over Lucie.

"For gracious sakes!" she exclaimed. "My precious little ladybird—a married woman! I can't decide if it's the worst disaster in the history of the universe, or a wonderful thing."

Jarvis Lorry chuckled and tugged on his little brown wig. "Come, come, my Pross. You decided a week ago that it's a good thing. Remember? As a banker, I can advise you. You made an investment in last week's decision, and you must not flipflop. We can all see how deeply happy Lucie and Charles are."

"What do you know about my ladybird's happiness?" Miss Pross demanded. "Have you cared for her since she was five years old? And what do you know about marriage—you, a bachelor!"

Mr. Lorry winked at the others. The longer he knew the members of the Manette household, the more he enjoyed teasing Miss Pross. "And what do *you* know about marriage, my dear *Miss* Pross? Anyway, try to recall that you've made your peace with the new situation."

Miss Pross eyed Charles with caution. She looked him up and down, from his black nose to the tip of his tail. "Well, I suppose you're all right," she concluded. "For gracious sakes, you're a good deal better than some!"

Charles stretched out his front legs and made a deep bow to Miss Pross. Everyone laughed, except Sydney Carton.

"Let's have tea," Lucie suggested. "Charles and I have brought back the most delicious biscuits from Wales."

While Miss Pross prepared the table, Jarvis Lorry whispered to Charles, "I'd like to speak with you privately."

Mr. Lorry and Charles stepped into the largest window alcove. Charles perched on a small chair. As they both gazed out the window, Mr. Lorry began.

"I believe you should know what happened here while you and Lucie were gone. Dr. Manette was very ill. But don't be alarmed. All is better than ever now. I will be brief—as a man of business should always be. And you must promise never to tell Lucie a word of what I say."

Charles nodded. His heart beat faster despite Mr. Lorry's promise of a good outcome.

Jarvis Lorry proceeded. "As soon as you and Lucie departed on your trip, the doctor fell into a kind of trance. He was confused and frightened. He paced up and down his consulting room—as if he were in a prison cell. When he wasn't pacing, he stood in a corner, holding his forehead. He wouldn't speak or go out."

Mr. Lorry glanced around to make sure no one was near the alcove. Then he continued.

"This went on for precisely nine and a half days. Bankers, of course, keep such precise records. Miss Pross and I never left the doctor alone. No one else saw him. The afternoon of the tenth day, he suddenly returned to his old self. It was like the sun appearing at the end of a violent storm. He's been perfectly fine since then."

"Does the doctor realize what happened?" Charles asked.

Mr. Lorry nodded. "He asked me to describe his state during those nine and a half days. I did so precisely. Then he told me that he would never again have such a breakdown."

"How does he know that?" Charles asked in an excited whisper. "How can he be sure?"

Jarvis Lorry leaned closer to Charles to reply. "Although

he's a man of science, the doctor could not explain it precisely. He knew only that he had nothing more to fear because he had lived through the worst! Apparently he discovered something the morning of your marriage. He said it was a secret he would never reveal as long as he lived."

Mr. Lorry straightened up just as Lucie called them all to tea.

"The news is good, Charles," Jarvis Lorry said. "Our Dr. Manette is well!"

Charles nodded, but he also shivered with guilt. *I caused the doctor's breakdown,* he thought. *For Dr. Manette, living through the worst was hearing my real name—Evrémonde!*

"Charles, dear," Lucie called gently, "come join us."

Charles looked at his graceful wife. Her soft hair reflected the afternoon light like strands of gold. Her lovely face filled with joy as she bent over her father's white head to pour his tea. Charles made a solemn promise to himself as he walked toward them.

"As long as we are all happy and well," he murmured, "I will never speak my real name to the doctor again."

Having made this vow, Charles felt completely light-hearted. He hopped onto the chair next to Lucie's and sniffed his tea. He flicked his tongue into the liquid to test its temperature. While he waited for it to cool, he took a biscuit with his teeth and began to nibble.

The loving group of friends and family spent two merry hours in conversation. Charles and Lucie described their travels in Wales. Everyone enjoyed the strong-tasting cheese, orange marmalade, and special biscuits—especially Charles.

"I believe there's no finer food in the world than a good biscuit," he declared.

After tea, Mr. Lorry hurried off to Tellson's bank to finish some business. Dr. Manette went into his consulting room to complete some reports. Miss Pross cleared away the tea dishes and then withdrew to her upstairs room. Lucie sat in the window alcove, looking at some watercolors of Wales that she had brought home as a souvenir. Sydney Carton joined her. Charles stretched out on the soft cushions of his favorite chair. Much happiness and many biscuits soon lulled him to sleep.

A few minutes later, a noise awakened Charles. Someone had sobbed. The sound lasted only an instant. Then the same voice—Sydney Carton's voice—spoke to Lucie.

"I want you to know," Sydney said, "that you have been the last dream of my soul. Since I've known you, I've had regrets about my lazy, drunken life. Before meeting you, I'd thought all those regrets had died."

Charles realized that Sydney Carton was making a deeply personal confession to Lucie. Charles's mind raced. *What shall I do? They don't understand how good my hearing is. I can hear every word they're whispering across the room. If I try to sneak out, they'll definitely see me. Sydney will be horribly*

embarrassed. He'll never be able to finish what he wants to tell Lucie. But if I stay, I can't help overhearing a most private conversation.

Charles decided it was best not to move. If he couldn't fall asleep again, he would try to ignore the words swirling around him.

"Oh, Mr. Carton," Lucie begged, "can't your regrets inspire a better life?" Tears shook her voice. "Can't you create a life more worthy of your talents and intelligence?"

"It's too late," Sydney Carton answered. "I shall never be better than I am. I shall sink lower and be worse."

"Please, Mr. Carton!" Lucie pleaded. "Don't I have any power for good over you?"

"In one way," Sydney whispered. His low voice was passionate. "In the future, think of me now and then and remember this—I would do anything for you, or for someone dear to you. I would give my life to keep a life you love beside you!"

Lucie sobbed quietly as Sydney stood to leave.

"I'm not worthy of your tears," he said. "But I will remember them at the moment of my death. Bless you for your compassion! When you see me next, I'll appear to be the same miserable individual whom you have known. But, for you, in my heart, I will always be the better man I am right now. Can you believe this?"

"Yes!" Lucie whispered between sobs.

"And will you promise to tell no one about this conversation—not even those you love most?"

"Yes."

"Good-bye," Sydney murmured.

Charles's muscles trembled beneath his fur. *Poor Sydney! Poor, sad, lost Sydney!*

The conversation had ended, so Charles pretended to awaken and stretch. He sat up. "Are you leaving already?" he asked Sydney.

Sydney looked calm and serious. He displayed none of his usual careless attitude.

"Yes, I'm leaving," he said. "Would you be willing to walk outside with me a little ways?"

"Of course," Charles said. He jumped off his chair and turned to Lucie. He pretended not to notice the tears on her cheeks. He grabbed his hat with his teeth and followed Sydney Carton out of the house.

Sydney remained silent, walking slowly, his head down. Charles walked along next to him.

"Mr. Darnay," Sydney said, "I wish that we might be friends."

Charles looked up at him in surprise. "I assumed we *were* friends."

"Those are just polite words," Sydney answered with his usual bluntness. "I'm talking about something else. I wish to apologize for rude remarks I made after your trial at the Old Bailey."

Once again, Charles was surprised. "Anything you said was very minor. Moreover, it counts for nothing when measured against the fact that you saved my life that day!"

Sydney shook his head. "That was mere lawyer's nonsense. I'm not sure I cared what happened to you that day. But that was the past. The present is very different."

Charles and Sydney walked on a little farther. Charles sniffed the air. His tail began to wag slowly. He felt more at ease with Sydney Carton than he ever had.

Sydney finally spoke. "I have a request. If you could stand to have a worthless fellow like myself around—"

"I don't consider you worthless," Charles interrupted.

"Well, I am," Sydney declared. "But I still have a request. I'd like permission to come and go uninvited—as a sort of privileged person in your household. You could think of me as an old piece of furniture. I wouldn't abuse the privilege. I doubt that I would use it even four times a year. I'd be satisfied just to know that I had permission."

Charles stopped walking and looked up into Sydney's serious face. "The permission is yours. I sincerely hope you'll use it often."

"Thank you, Charles," Sydney said. "May I say your name in that informal way?"

"By this time, Sydney, I should think so!"

Charles held out his paw and shook Sydney's hand. After a few moments, Sydney abruptly turned away and crossed the road.

Charles watched him depart. "I wish you well, my friend," he murmured. He turned in the opposite direction and walked back to the house.

Charles nudged open the sitting room door with his nose. The room was empty. He trotted up another flight of stairs to the rooms that now belonged to him and Lucie. Miss Pross had moved to the highest floor of the house.

"Lucie?" Charles asked as he pushed open their bedroom door.

Lucie was arranging the brushes for Charles's fur on the dresser top. She hurried over to him, knelt, and put her arms around his neck.

"Charles," she said, "we must always treat poor Sydney Carton with respect. And we must be forgiving of his faults."

Charles watched a single tear drop from each of her blue eyes. He gently wiped them off her cheeks with his paw.

Lucie continued. "Mr. Carton has a sensitive heart, which is badly wounded. Yet I know he's capable of good actions—even selfless actions."

Charles placed his front paws on Lucie's shoulders. "I agree with you, my darling," he said.

Lucie hugged him. "Let's always remember how strong we are in our happiness—and how lucky!"

The young couple looked out the window. The setting sun cast its rose-colored light over the trees, the road, and the quiet neighborhood. The light seemed to expand and include Lucie, Charles, and their future together.

"I can almost see the years slipping by," Charles whispered, ". . . happy years." He held Lucie even closer. "What do you think will happen to us, my love? What do you think our lives will be like years from now?"

Chapter Ten

The light of happiness shone steadily on the old-fashioned gray house in the Soho neighborhood of London for eight years. In 1789, Dr. Manette still took care of his patients. Charles taught his students. Jarvis Lorry and Sydney Carton tended to their professions—Mr. Lorry with the extreme care of a banker, Mr. Carton with complete carelessness. Miss Pross took care of the house and everyone's business. Around them all, Lucie wove ties of affection and loyalty like a golden web.

Charles and Lucie provided the household with its most important and welcome addition—a child. Their daughter, Lizzie, celebrated her sixth birthday in 1789. Lizzie had her mother's golden curls and her father's deep brown eyes. She had smiles, stories, laughter, and games for everyone—but most of all for Sydney Carton. Whenever he appeared at the door, Lizzie ran to hug him. During his visits, nothing pleased her more than playing with her toys under his quiet gaze. And nothing soothed him more than watching her.

Thus, Charles Darnay and Dr. Manette created a safe place for themselves and their loved ones in their adopted city of London. Meanwhile, across the English Channel, in their native city of Paris, the most intense kind of fire had started to burn—the fire of revolution.

"Dr. Manette! Charles! Come quickly! I mean—here I come! I have news!"

Jarvis Lorry clambered up the stairs inside the gray house with surprising speed for a man of seventy. It was a warm summer day in 1789. He plunged into the sitting room, breathing hard. His little brown wig had slipped down over his forehead.

Lucie, who had been reading, stood up. Her book fell from her hands. Charles, who had been rolling on the floor with Lizzie, sat up. He placed a paw on Lizzie's shoulder so she wouldn't be frightened. Dr. Manette rushed out of his consulting room. They all stared at Jarvis Lorry.

Mr. Lorry quickly straightened his wig. Facing them all, he made his announcement. "The poor people of Paris have revolted! They attacked the Bastille prison! They killed the prison warden and cut off his head! The Bastille has been torn down to the ground!"

"Father!" Lucie cried.

Everyone turned to Dr. Manette. The color had drained from his face. One hand gripped the door frame. A moment passed. He shook his head and shoulders. When he spoke, his voice sounded normal.

"Please don't be alarmed. It was just the shock of the news. The Bastille gone! As a former prisoner of that dungeon, I want to say this is a great event. But the violence! I fear that kind of violence."

"As a banker, I agree completely," Mr. Lorry said. He was still breathing hard. He pulled out a linen handkerchief and wiped perspiration off his face. Lucie motioned to him to sit down.

Charles paced across the room. His nails clicked sharply on the floor. He knew Lucie could see how tense his muscles were under his fur.

"I've always been afraid this would happen," Charles said. "The aristocrats treated the working people so brutally. They starved them, robbed them, and murdered them. They wasted every resource. They caused the nation of France to go broke. Now the ordinary people have risen up against the harsh rulers. But some of the ordinary people will use the same brutal methods. They will seek revenge."

"You're right, Charles," Dr. Manette said. "When I was locked away in the Bastille, I, too, thought I wanted revenge. It's a dangerous desire."

The door to the sitting room opened again—slowly this time.

"Mr. Carton!" Lizzie exclaimed. She skipped over to Sydney Carton while he stood in the doorway. He bent down so that her arms could wrap around his neck. His eyes smiled at her, although the rest of his expression didn't change.

"Have you heard the news, Sydney?" Charles asked. "There's been an uprising in Paris."

Sydney nodded. "Not only in Paris. Groups of peasants in the countryside are burning down châteaus. There are reports of murder and torture." He walked toward his favorite spot in the window alcove. "I suppose some peasants are behaving like their masters. In any case, the masters are getting out of France as fast as they can—like rats fleeing a sinking ship."

Charles's ears pricked up. "Did you happen to hear the name of any particular château?"

Sydney shrugged. "They say a big stone place, less than a day's ride from Paris, made the nicest blaze."

"Did anyone mention the owner's name?" Charles asked.

Sydney stared at Charles for a moment. He shrugged

again. "A marquis, I think. The last descendant of one of the old families. Yes—the Marquis Saint Evrémonde."

Charles's heart pounded in his chest. His mouth opened. *C'est moi!* he thought. *That's me!* He couldn't stop himself from glancing at Dr. Manette. Their eyes met for an instant. Charles clamped his strong jaw shut and turned away.

Three more years slipped by. They were years of peace and simple pleasures for the Manette household. Lizzie celebrated three more birthdays surrounded by family and friends. She turned nine in 1792. The relationship between Charles and Lucie grew closer each year. They never stopped marveling at their good fortune.

Yet happiness within the Manette household was not perfect. While the family enjoyed peace at home, the conflict in France grew more fierce. Each day brought more disturbing news. The fury of the revolution caused equally furious reactions.

By 1791, the revolutionary government had stripped all aristocrats of their titles of nobility, as well as their special privileges. Some of the aristocrats who fled France organized an army. They planned to invade their own country and crush the revolution. They got help from aristocrats in other European countries. Spies worked everywhere. One plot followed another.

In 1792, more violent revolutionaries seized power in France. Mobs of people often took the law into their own hands. Some wanted to kill every aristocrat. They began to throw thousands of people into prison.

All the while, the revolutionary leaders fought among themselves for power. Whenever one group seized control, another one soon toppled the first group. The new leaders imprisoned the former ones. The extremists declared war on everyone—inside and outside France—who opposed them. Violence and terror triumphed.

Late one afternoon in mid-August 1792, Charles Darnay hurried across a busy street in the heart of London. His compact, furred body darted among carriages, carts, horses, and bustling people. He headed straight for a window at the front of the London office of Tellson's bank. When he reached the building, he stood on his hind legs and stretched his front legs up to the windowsill. He read a sign posted on the glass:

LATEST NEWS FROM FRANCE
THE REVOLUTIONARY GOVERNMENT HAS SEIZED
THE PROPERTY OF ALL ARISTOCRATS.

Charles continued to stare at the sign, but he no longer saw the words. Instead, he pictured the Evrémonde lands in France and the tiny village with the old fountain. He thought of Monsieur Gabelle, the good man who had managed the land for the past twelve years.

"I must get in touch with Gabelle," Charles murmured. "I must make sure he's all right."

Charles dropped his front paws to the ground and walked into Tellson's bank. The wood-paneled main room was crowded with people—almost all of them French aristocrats. Since 1789, Tellson's had been the main meeting place for aristocrats who had fled the revolution. Those who managed to take money out of France did their banking at Tellson's. Those who lost their wealth borrowed money there. Everyone exchanged news and gossip about the revolution. They whispered about plots and spies. The bank posted the most important news of the day in its window for passersby to see.

Charles made his way through the maze of desks and clerks' tables. He dodged legs covered with silk stockings and feet wearing satin shoes. With so many different perfumes in the air, his sensitive nose twitched constantly.

"A-choo!" Charles rubbed his nose with one paw. *I'm just as allergic to these people in England as I was to them in France*, he thought.

Charles caught snatches of conversation as he moved along.

"—like to kill every revolutionary myself—"

"—worthless low-class people—"

"—avenge our ancient honor—"

Charles reached the far end of the room. His sharp eyes caught the equally keen gaze of Jarvis Lorry, who was sitting behind a desk.

"Charles, my friend!" Mr. Lorry said. He turned and shook Charles's paw.

"I wanted to say farewell before you leave for Paris tonight," Charles said. "But I must say . . . although you're very young at heart . . . I do wonder—"

Mr. Lorry chuckled. "You think I'm too old to undertake this journey, right?"

Charles sighed. "We both know how dangerous France is now—especially Paris."

Jarvis Lorry nodded. "But as an employee of Tellson's bank for more than fifty years, I must go. There are hundreds of important documents in our Paris office. If they fall into the wrong hands, many lives will be at risk. I know which documents to destroy and which to bury in the ground until safer times."

"Ah, burying things in the ground," Charles said. "That's a job I could help you do." Without thinking, he added, "I often wish I could go to Paris."

"You!" Mr. Lorry kept his voice low, but he sounded shocked. "You're a French aristocrat by birth! How can you utter such a wish? In Paris, you'd be like a canary locked in a cage with a hungry cat!"

"That's an ugly picture!" Charles muttered. He shook his head. "Still, I can't help but think that I might be of use in Paris. I've always had sympathy for the poor. I've tried to help them. Perhaps some revolutionaries would listen to me. Perhaps I could convince them to stop the violence. Perhaps—"

"For shame!" Mr. Lorry hissed. "Think of Lucie! Think of Lizzie! Suppose something happened to you! Every gate into Paris is guarded by people who hate all aristocrats. There are dozens of checkpoints on every road. Almost anyone could have you thrown into prison. No laws would protect you."

"Pardon me, Mr. Lorry," someone said. Another employee of Tellson's bank stepped up to his desk. "Have you been able to deliver that letter?"

Mr. Lorry reached into one of the many packets of papers

on his desk. He took out a soiled, unopened letter. "I'm afraid not," he said. "No one knows where to find this gentleman." He pointed to a name on the front of the letter.

Charles could read the writing. His mouth dropped open.

To Monsieur, formerly known as the Marquis Saint Evrémonde of France. Sent care of Tellson's bank in London, England. Urgent!

A bell jingled to announce that the bank was closing for the day. Jarvis Lorry walked to the front of the main room, carrying the letter. Charles followed him.

As clients filed out the door, Mr. Lorry showed the letter to each one. Every aristocrat from France recognized the name on the letter and had a comment to make.

"Traitor to his name! He threw away his family's estate. He just tossed it to the low-class poor folk!"

"I don't know where he is—but if I did, I'd spit in his face!"

"That's the nephew of the murdered Marquis Saint Evrémonde. His uncle was a jewel—a true aristocrat. The nephew is scum!"

"They say he was ruined by those filthy new ideas of freedom and equality! What garbage!"

"I'd call him a yellow-bellied coward."

"*Mais oui!* But, yes, of course! They say he left France hidden in a hay wagon—with his head buried and his legs sticking straight up!"

Charles could restrain himself no longer. "That is not true!" His white, furred body was shaking all over. His black nostrils flared. He knew that in a moment he would be snarling out loud.

A tall Frenchman in a long, powdered wig and a blue silk coat stepped back from the door. He looked down his nose and waved a lace handkerchief in Charles's direction. "And what do *you* know about it, *s'il vous plaît,* if you please?" he asked.

"I'm acquainted with the fellow," Charles replied.

"Well, *quel dommage*—what a shame for you!" The Frenchman sneered. "We can always judge a Frenchman by the company he keeps." He strutted out the door.

Charles tried to calm himself. *I'm letting these aristocrats ruffle my fur like a bunch of whining cats.*

Mr. Lorry interrupted Charles's thoughts. "I'm relieved to hear that you know this Marquis Saint Evrémonde," he said. "Could you deliver the letter to him? I have only a few minutes to finish getting ready for my journey to Paris. You know how I am—I don't want any loose ends flapping around after I leave here."

"Certainly," Charles said. He took the letter with his teeth and slipped it into his waistcoat pocket. He wished Mr. Lorry a safe and successful trip.

Charles left Tellson's bank and rushed along the crowded streets. A few minutes later, he arrived at the Temple—a group of buildings, connected by paths and courtyards, where many lawyers lived and worked. In one of the quiet courtyards, he tore the letter open with his teeth and began to read:

Prison of the Abbaye, Paris
June 21, 1792

Most Generous Monsieur Charles,

I, Gabelle, your old and loyal servant, wait for death in this horrible prison. A month ago, the villagers on your land captured me and burned my house to the ground. With beatings and curses, they forced me to march to Paris.

The Revolutionary Tribunal here has condemned me to death. Why? They claim I betrayed the revolution by working for an aristocrat! For you! The judges refuse to believe that I tried to help the peasants upon orders from you. They ask me again and again, "Where is this aristocrat? Why isn't he here to defend you?"

And I ask heaven the same thing every hour of every day. "Where is he? Why won't he save the life of his loyal servant?"

Most Generous Monsieur Charles—for the love of justice, for the honor of your name, help me! Be true to me, as I have been true to you!

> *Your suffering servant—*
> *Théophile Gabelle*

An immense wave of pain and distress swept over Charles. He couldn't catch his breath. His four legs wobbled. *Good, faithful Gabelle is about to lose his life—because of me!*

Charles bent his head down until his ears almost touched the ground. The dizziness quickly passed. He began to pace along the courtyard path—up and back, up and back. He felt himself being pulled in opposite directions by two cities, two loyalties, two duties, and two loves.

Words throbbed in his brain. *London. Paris. Loyalty to family. Loyalty to a friend in trouble. Duty as a husband and as a father. Duty as a gentleman. Love of Lucie and Lizzie—the most precious beings in the world. Love of justice and honor.*

Charles walked faster and faster. The muscles of his neck bulged until they were twice their normal size. Blood rushed to his head. His soft ears became rigid.

He pictured Lucie and Lizzie alone in the gray house in Soho. *Suppose I never return to them!* Charles groaned out loud, as if he were being torn apart.

He thought of France. Centuries of suffering and injustice,

the explosion of rage, destruction, murder. How would it end? He pictured centuries more of suffering. Could he do something? Could he possibly help to stop the violence?

A voice inside Charles's head seemed to warn him. *Don't act out of pride. Why should anyone in France listen to you? You haven't done anything special. Don't act out of guilt. Going to Paris will not erase the centuries of Evrémonde crimes.*

Charles stopped pacing. He looked straight ahead. He thought once more of golden-haired Lucie and Lizzie. He raised one paw, as if to step toward them. . . .

He felt a strange force, pulling at him like a powerful magnet. He couldn't step forward. Instead, his raised paw swatted the air, as if swatting aside the voice inside his head.

Charles's paw dropped to the ground. He turned slowly and faced in the opposite direction. He spoke to himself—and to fate—in a clear voice.

"I leave for Paris tonight."

What a nose for trouble! Charles Darnay can smell it all the way across the English Channel. Of course, his mistake in this case is to follow his nose.

Back in Oakdale, I'm about to make the same mistake.

87

Chapter Eleven

"I smell trouble." Wishbone stood in the hallway of the house, sniffing deeply, carefully, and with great suspicion. He tried to ignore the large floppy bow that Emily and Tina had attached to his collar ten minutes earlier. "The canine commando stands above such small concerns."

After sniffing once more, Wishbone stretched up to his full height.

"Commando Wishbone prepares to flush out alien intruders. He skillfully identifies ground zero—the enemy's position. It is . . . the kitchen! Commando Wishbone will now launch his mission. Good luck to him!"

Wishbone moved toward the kitchen. He slid his paws silently along the wood floor. As soon as he reached the door, he spotted something on the kitchen floor.

"Drops of a strange red liquid. Highly suspicious, and probably lethal."

He approached the drops with caution, lowered his head, and sniffed.

"Cranberry-apple. Not a good sign. Aha! More drops by the refrigerator. The trail is still wet."

With his nose down, Wishbone circled the kitchen,

keeping close to the cabinets. He passed the refrigerator, the sink, the stove. He rounded the corner, heading toward his own eating place.

"*Agh-h-h-h!* There they are! In my private dining room! Violating every rule known to civilized pups!"

Emily and Tina were sitting on the floor near Wishbone's bowl. Emily was pouring cranberry-apple juice from a large pitcher. Tina was holding up a china cup. The cup overflowed. The juice spilled onto the floor, making the red puddle there even larger.

"Wishbone wants to come to our tea party," Emily said. "Let's give him some tea."

Wishbone shook his head hard and fast. "No, thank you. I'm not thirsty." Emily kept pouring. "Hey, you'd better be careful with that!" Wishbone yelped. "Oh, great—you've turned my dining area into a swamp."

Tina giggled. "Oops!"

Emily laughed and grabbed Wishbone's blue chew toy, which was lying under the table. Waving it in the air, she ran out of the kitchen. Tina jumped up and ran after her.

Wishbone barked. "Hey, that's mine! You come back here with that! There are laws about personal property!" He dashed after them.

The girls raced into the study.

Wishbone followed them at top speed. "You put that down right now! That is not a toy! I mean it!"

Emily tossed the toy to Tina. Tina let it fall on the floor. "Let's play trampoline," she said.

The girls climbed onto Wishbone's big red armchair. They began to jump up and down on the cushion.

"We can fly!" Emily shouted. "We can fly!"

Wishbone leaped for his toy and snatched it up in his teeth. *First, I've got to secure my valuables*, he thought. He hid the toy under the couch. *Maybe Commando Wishbone should stay in the safety of this bunker for a while.*

"Watch us fly!" Tina shouted.

Wishbone groaned and stuck his head out. "That's my chair—not a trampoline!"

The girls jumped off the chair and ran out of the room. Wishbone emerged from under the couch.

"Is it time to put an end to this mission? No! Commando Wishbone pursues his goal doggedly. He evaluates the situation. His entire home is under attack. The enemy is basically out of control. He needs an updated plan. Something bold, brash, brilliant. Hmmm . . . Oh, yes, he's got it!"

Wishbone jumped onto the couch, stood on his hind legs, and stared outside through the windowpane.

He shouted, "Help! Joe! David! Anybody!"

After a minute of useless barking, Wishbone jumped off the couch.

"So much for that plan. Commando Wishbone is on his own and must again take charge. He will subdue the enemy. But first he must *find* the enemy."

That said, Wishbone marched out of the study. He pricked up his ears.

"Aha! The enemy has occupied the high ground—upstairs."

Wishbone ran over to the bottom of the staircase. He looked up.

Emily and Tina stood at the top of the stairs. Each girl held a new roll of white toilet paper.

Wishbone shook his head wildly. "No—not the toilet paper!" He waved his front paws in the air. "Ellen hates it when anybody messes with the toilet paper. Believe me—I know. Girls, girls, this is not good."

It was no use. The girls tossed the rolls of toilet paper

high into the air and let them bounce down the stairs, unwinding along the way.

Being home alone with Emily and Tina is like a nightmare—only worse, because I can't wake up.

Charles Darnay finds a similar situation in France. Every day for a week he is awakened into the same nightmare. He can't get out of it, and every day it grows more frightening. . . .

Chapter Twelve

"Wake up, aristocrat! In the name of the revolution, wake up!"

Charles groaned as rough hands shook his aching shoulders and jabbed his furred hide. Even rougher voices shouted at him in French.

Where am I? he wondered. After a moment's confusion, he remembered. He had fallen asleep on a dirty bed in the back room of a guardhouse. The guardhouse was located at the edge of a small town on the road leading to Paris.

Charles sat up quickly and shook dust and bits of straw out of his fur. He flicked a flea off one ear and quickly brushed his crumpled, unwashed shirt. A single candle provided the only light. *It's the middle of the night,* he thought.

Three men stood over him. Despite the dim light, Charles recognized the town's gatekeeper as one of them. All three had the red-stocking cap worn by many revolutionary citizens. They all folded down the pointed end of the cap and fastened it with an ornament of blue, white, and red—the colors of revolutionary France. They carried muskets and swords. Each had tied a blue, white, and red scarf around his neck. The rest of the clothes on their lean bodies were practically rags.

"Aristocrat," the gatekeeper said, "I'm sending you directly to Paris with these two citizens as your escorts. They will make sure you get there."

"I want nothing more than to reach Paris," Charles said. "But I don't need escorts. I've come to France freely and openly as a Frenchman. I can continue traveling on my own."

"Silence!" one of the other men growled. He slammed the butt of his musket hard against the side of the bed. "You're an aristocrat, and all aristocrats must have escorts."

"And aristocrats must pay for their escorts," the gatekeeper added. "Finish getting dressed. You're leaving right away."

Charles picked up his coat with his teeth and pulled it on. Seizing the handle of his small suitcase in his mouth, he followed the men out of the guardhouse. Two horses stood saddled and waiting.

Don't worry, Charles told himself. *These people are no worse than the many others you've met up with in France.*

Groups of men and women had stopped him a hundred times so far. They appeared without warning on every road. They guarded every village and town. They always wore the red caps of the revolution and carried weapons. They always called one another "citizen" and "patriot." They no longer thought of themselves as subjects of the French king. They wanted to be free and equal citizens of the republic.

These citizens always demanded to see Charles's papers. They searched for his name on their lists. They asked dozens of questions. They called him "aristocrat" and "enemy of the revolution." They also called him "emigrant," which meant he was a French person who had left France to live elsewhere. The trip from the coast at Calais to Paris had turned into an endless nightmare. He had been traveling a week, and Paris was still a long way off.

"Hurry up, aristocrat!" the first escort shouted. He grabbed Charles by the shoulders of his coat and lifted him onto the saddle of a horse. "You're riding with me." He swung into the saddle behind Charles and gripped him by the collar with one hand.

Charles's fur bristled, but he said nothing. Instead, he turned to the gatekeeper. "May I have my letter?"

The gatekeeper nodded and gave Charles the letter from Monsieur Gabelle. Charles tucked it carefully into the deepest pocket of his *coat*. He used the letter to explain why he had returned to France. Gabelle had addressed it to the Marquis Saint Evrémonde. *How strange to be called "Evrémonde" by everyone—and not "Darnay,"* Charles thought.

"You'd better hurry up," the gatekeeper said to the two escorts. "There are other citizens demanding to deal with this Evrémonde—if you know what I mean."

"They can do what they want with this Evrémonde, for all I care," the first escort muttered.

"Let him pay up for our services," the second escort said. "The work of the revolution must go on."

Charles paid the gatekeeper the large sum of money required. The horses turned and started up the road at a fast clip. Charles's thoughts hammered in his brain to the hammering rhythm of the horses' hooves.

I'm trapped—trapped on this horse, trapped on this road, trapped in France. Every door has shut behind me. Charles looked straight ahead, as if looking directly into his future. *There's only one way I'll ever get out of France. The revolutionary government in Paris must declare that I am a good citizen.*

The horses passed scattered huts and wilted fields on the outskirts of the town. Charles still felt hopeful. *With Monsieur Gabelle's help, I can prove that I've hurt no one. I can show that I never collected taxes from the peasants, that I—*

Loud cries startled the horses and riders. A group of

about twenty citizens charged out from behind a farmhouse, waving weapons and shouting.

"Down with the aristocrat Evrémonde!"

"Down with the emigrant!"

Charles realized that news about him must have spread from the last checkpoint.

They surrounded the horses. By the light of their torches, Charles could see hatred in the peoples' eyes. He could smell the desire for violence rising up from their skin. A man holding up a blacksmith's hammer sprang forward and tried to grab the bridle of the horse that Charles rode.

The second escort spoke in a calm voice. "Citizens, let the aristocrat be as he is. He will be judged soon enough in Paris."

"Aye!" the blacksmith shrieked. "Judged—and then condemned as a traitor!"

Charles's need to explain and defend himself overcame his horror of the mob. He took a deep breath and raised one of his front paws. "Friends, you have been lied to. I'm not a traitor. I—"

"He does not speak the truth!" the blacksmith shouted. "Evrémonde is a traitor since the new law! His life is no longer his own!"

Crying "Aye!" and "Down with Evrémonde!," the people pressed forward. Charles dug his front paws deep into the horse's mane and prepared to hold on for dear life. The first escort sat on the saddle behind him without doing or saying anything to help Charles.

"No, not yet!" the second escort shouted. "The revolution will judge Evrémonde in Paris!"

He kicked his horse into motion. The other horse followed. As the animals plunged forward, the mob fell back. A hand grabbed at Charles's coat, but his paws held onto the horse's mane. A moment later, the horses made their way

out of the crowd. They galloped down the road and didn't let up their pace until the danger was past.

Charles shivered in the chilly night air. It took ten minutes for his breathing to return to a normal rate. But when he allowed himself to think about his situation, his heart began to pound again. He turned to the second escort. "What is this new law the blacksmith mentioned? Why did he call me a traitor?"

The escort answered without looking at Charles. "Everyone says the government is going to pass a law that declares all emigrants must be forced to leave France forever. Any emigrant who returns will be condemned to death. Emigrants are likely to be spies."

Charles's whiskers quivered. "But the law hasn't been passed yet."

The escort behind Charles laughed. "What difference does that make, emigrant?"

A light rain began to fall. After an hour, the rain came down harder. The dirt road turned to mud. The horses slogged along, tired and cold. The wetness soaked through Charles's clothes. Drops trickled down from his ears, soft nose, and long muzzle. The miserable weather drenched his spirits. For the first time, he admitted the truth to himself. *By stepping onto French soil, I've stepped into a death trap!*

Dawn came. In the weak light, Charles made out the scorched remains of burned buildings. They stopped at the next town. The escorts made arrangements for Charles to rest in the guardhouse there until evening.

"I have orders to deliver you to Paris alive," the second escort said. "We'll meet fewer citizen patrols if we ride at night."

Charles took off his wet clothes in a back room and lay down on the dirt floor. Every muscle beneath his furred hide ached. He covered his eyes with his front paws. The image of the house in Soho took shape in his mind. *Lucie, my love, my life! Lizzie! Dr. Manette!*

Charles moaned when he thought of his last night in England. He had secretly packed the small suitcase and hidden it in the stairwell of the house. He told Lucie he had to take care of an errand in town and would return home late. He nuzzled his head against her smooth cheek one last time, then left the house. Just before boarding a hired coach, he wrote her a letter, explaining his sudden departure for Paris. He promised to return soon.

"Soon!" Charles murmured. "It's already late!" With the image of his wife and child in his mind, he fell asleep.

After one more long night of riding, Charles and his escorts arrived at the walls that enclosed the capital city of Paris. Groups of soldiers and citizen patrols guarded the gates. Charles noticed that the guards let peasants and crafts people enter the city without much delay. But leaving Paris was another matter. The citizen patrols examined every cart, every wagon, and every person, as if each was a threat to the success of the revolution.

"Hurry up, aristocrat!" The escort sitting behind Charles jumped off the horse and pulled Charles to the ground. The other escort took his suitcase. They pushed through the crowd around the gate and entered the guardhouse. As Charles squeezed by, the citizens in their red caps pointed at him and whispered.

Inside the guardhouse, a dozen soldiers and citizens stood around a large desk where an officer in uniform sat. Piles of documents and a big book of names lay on the desk.

Charles and his escorts stood in front of the desk until the officer finally looked at Charles. "Where are this prisoner's papers?"

Again the fur on Charles's back bristled. "I am not a prisoner. I have come to France freely as a citizen."

"Where are this prisoner's papers?" the officer repeated.

"Give him your letter," the first escort growled.

Charles handed Gabelle's letter to the officer.

The officer read the letter and then addressed the escorts. "This is the emigrant Evrémonde—formerly called the Marquis Saint Evrémonde?"

First there was a gasp. Then murmurs rose from all the listeners. The escorts nodded. The officer quickly filled out a short form. It was a receipt for Charles—as if he were a sack of wheat or a side of beef. The escorts took the receipt and departed.

The officer began filling out another form. Without looking up, he fired questions at Charles.

"Where do you now live, Evrémonde?"

"England."

"Are you married?"

"Yes."

"Where were you married?"

"England."

"Where is your wife now?"

"England."

The officer finished writing. "Emigrant Evrémonde, you are assigned to the prison called La Force."

Charles's four legs became rigid. "Prison! For what crime? Under what law?"

"We have new laws, and therefore new crimes, since you were last in France," the officer said. A hard little smile twisted his lips. "Especially for emigrants."

"But—"

Two armed citizen guards stepped up to Charles. Like the citizens who stopped Charles on the road, these citizens in Paris had declared themselves guards. They, too, wore red caps with their ordinary clothes. The officer handed one of them the form. "Bring back a receipt for the prisoner from La Force."

Charles had no choice but to step toward the door. As he did, a tall, hefty woman blocked the way. Her features were bold but perfectly still. She wore large earrings and a scarf wrapped around her head to which she had sewn a blue, white, and red ribbon. She had knotted a red scarf around her neck. A dagger was thrust beneath the sash around her waist. A pistol was tucked into the front folds of her dress. She was knitting a long scarf decorated with a pattern of strange symbols. The scarf lay folded in a basket that she carried on her arm. Her knitting needles danced back and forth as her eyes studied Charles's face. She took in every marking, every bit of fur, every whisker.

A shiver ran down Charles's spine as he stared back at her. *I've seen her before! But where?*

"I will accompany this prisoner and the citizen guards to La Force prison," the woman said. She spoke to the officer with the tone of a general.

The officer nodded. "As you wish, Citizen Defarge."

The knitting woman led the way out of the guardhouse and through the gates into the streets of Paris. Charles trotted between the two armed guards. Inside the crowded city, an occasional red-capped citizen shook a fist in Charles's direction or rattled a sword. But for the most part, no one paid attention to their little procession.

They must see dozens of prisoners under guard every day, Charles thought. As his paws clicked along the uneven paving stones, he recalled the last time he had walked the streets of Paris. *The city has changed so much in twelve years! No gold-painted carriages, no aristocrats in satin coats and lace cuffs, no taffeta parasols or diamond-studded canes. Everyone is wearing simple clothes. The only decorations are scarves and sashes of blue, white, and red; daggers; and pistols!*

"Paris has changed, eh?" The knitting woman stepped between Charles and one of the guards. Charles felt the rough hem of her skirt brush against his fur as they walked along. His fur stood on end. "A lot has happened in twelve years, eh?"

Charles looked up at her in surprise. "How did you know I was last here twelve years ago?"

The woman walked, knitted, and never looked at Charles. "Do you remember the little square with the fountain in the Saint Antoine neighborhood? Do you remember the carriage—your uncle's, wasn't it, eh? And what about that little boy—broken like a twig under the carriage wheels? Remember, eh?"

Charles froze. "I recall that awful day. Were you there, too?"

"Move on!" a guard snarled. He butted Charles's shoulder with his musket.

Charles continued to walk, but his eyes remained fixed on the knitting woman. A bitter smile pulled at her lips.

"Was I—Madame Defarge—there? Why shouldn't I have been? I run the wine shop in the square. As I remember, you took shelter in my doorway."

For a moment, in Charles's mind, the Paris of 1792 became the Paris of 1780. He was standing in the doorway of the wine shop. The same woman stood next to him, knitting. She was memorizing every feature of his face. She was asking his name.

"Evrémonde!"

Charles snapped back to the present.

"Evrémonde, I want to show you something," Madame Defarge said. "Look!"

She nudged Charles with her foot, and they walked to the edge of an immense public square. Charles knew the place well. He realized immediately that the centerpiece of the square—a statue of one of the French kings—was gone.

"Do you see our new *statue*, Evrémonde?" Madame

Defarge pointed to a tall contraption mounted on a high wooden platform.

Charles felt his blood run cold. The hide beneath his fur felt as if it had been pricked by a thousand pins. He couldn't take his eyes off the strange device.

It was a simple structure. Two sturdy posts rose to a height of about twelve feet—like a vertical pair of tracks. Suspended between the two posts was a gleaming metal blade—like a giant ax. Far below the blade, near the bottom of the posts, was a stock—a vertical wooden frame with a hole in the middle. The frame would lock around a person's neck and hold the neck directly below the blade.

"La guillotine!" Madame Defarge said softly. "The queen of the revolution! See how modern and humane she is. The blade is very heavy. It comes down swiftly. It cuts off the head from the neck in an instant."

Charles was having a hard time swallowing. He rubbed his neck with a front paw. The strong muscles under his white fur suddenly felt delicate, even fragile. Madame Defarge smiled.

They arrived at La Force prison a few minutes later. Charles looked up at the double iron doors. *In a moment, these doors will shut behind me. Then no one in the world who cares about me will know where I am. I will be lost to those I love.*

Charles quickly turned to Madame Defarge. "I know you hate me. But I'm forced anyway to ask you for one favor. Will you inform Mr. Jarvis Lorry—the Tellson's bank officer here in Paris—that I am imprisoned in La Force?"

Madame Defarge placed her knitting in her basket. Her dark eyes met Charles's eyes. "I will do nothing for you, Evrémonde." She turned and walked away.

Chapter Thirteen

The citizen guards led Charles to a small window near the prison door. They handed his documents to the jailer, who sat on the other side of the window.

"Another guest for my little hotel!" the jailer said, laughing at his own cruel joke. "We're almost full here. What this revolution needs is more prisons."

One of Charles's guards grinned. "Don't worry, citizen. We'll have plenty of room when the guillotine begins to work full-time. Prisoners without heads don't need beds!"

The guards and the jailer laughed long and hard. Charles's muzzle wrinkled into a grimace of disgust.

Still laughing, the jailer handed the guards a receipt. Then he unbolted the heavy iron doors. They opened just enough for Charles to squeeze through. Once inside the doors, he turned to see the open sky and the world of freedom one last time.

The doors clanged shut.

La Force prison was filthy and dark. Charles followed the jailer along narrow corridors, through vaulted hallways, up and down spiraling staircases. Every passage began and ended with an iron door. The jailer rattled his heavy mass of keys. The doors slammed shut behind Charles.

The humid air stank of the odor of unwashed bodies and spoiled food. The stone walls gave off a foul-smelling moisture. Charles found the smells overpowering. He swayed on his four paws. Just when he thought he would collapse, the jailer stopped at a low door.

"This is your new home," he said. He turned a key in the lock and swung the door open.

Charles stepped inside. The jailer immediately withdrew. Charles called after him, "Can I buy pen and paper?"

The jailer called back, "For now, all you'll be buying is your food." With that remark, the jailer disappeared.

Charles examined his cell. It was cold and damp, but not completely dark. The furnishings included a small table, a chair, and a straw mattress. He sniffed and then peered closely at the mattress. *Ugh! Bedmates by the thousands. And all of them with six legs!*

Charles slowly walked the length and width of the cell. A layer of filth on the stone floor muffled the sound of his paws. He measured the cell as he walked.

"Four paces by four and a half," he murmured. "Four paces by four and a half." He walked up and down the cell again . . . and again . . . and again. "Four by four and a half. Four by four and a half." He walked faster. He counted his steps in a louder voice to drown out his growing despair. He counted still louder to keep a sob from escaping his throat.

Charles walked and counted for hours. He walked and counted until his mind was numb. He walked and counted until his four legs could carry him no longer. He dropped onto the straw mattress and slept.

When he awakened, early morning light was filtering through a grate high in the wall. Charles rolled off the mattress and shook himself as hard as he could. Then he nosed around the floor of the cell until he found a sharp pebble. He

picked up the pebble in his teeth and scratched a short vertical line on the wall.

"One day of my life lost in prison," he said.

Nine more days passed. Charles made a new mark on the wall every morning. Around noon on the tenth day, he heard noises in the distance. His ears pricked up. He heard shouting, rapid footsteps, and iron doors banging open and shut. The faraway noises grew louder and louder, like the gathering of a fierce storm.

Charles stood in the middle of his cell, his body rigid. *What is it? A prison uprising? A riot?*

The noise finally reached the passage outside his cell. A key clinked in the lock, and the door swung open. Four citizen guards rushed in. They carried knives, swords, and hatchets.

Charles gasped. He saw blood on the weapons.

The guards grabbed Charles by his front paws and dragged him into the passage. They pulled him along corridors and up and down stairs. The shouting and banging grew louder. These sounds were mixed with terrible screams. Pushing through one last door, they emerged into a large vaulted room.

The guards shoved Charles into the middle of a huddled mass of people—men, women, some children—all prisoners. Dozens of armed citizen guards stood over them. A smaller group of citizens sat behind a long wooden table at one end of the room. Charles noticed one head wrapped in a scarf—and a pair of flashing knitting needles.

Madame Defarge!

Charles watched the scene and quickly understood what was happening. A mob of angry people had decided to put all the prisoners on trial. The group at the table played the role of jury. They called out names—one by one—that were listed in a large book. Each prisoner who was called would step forward and answer two or three questions. The jury would immediately deliver a verdict. They shouted "Condemned!" in almost all cases. Guards then dragged the prisoner from the room. On rare occasions, the jury shouted "Free the prisoner!"

Aside from outbursts of shouting by the jury and guards, the room was quiet. Charles realized that all the wild cries and terrible shrieks were coming from the corridors and from outside the prison.

One young woman sat on the floor next to Charles with her hands over her face. Charles gently put a paw on her arm to comfort her. "Can you tell me where the condemned are being taken?" he asked.

She nodded and whispered, "Look out the window—if you dare!"

Taking care not to be noticed, Charles moved through the crowd of prisoners. He made his way to a stone bench below a barred window. "*Pardonnez-moi*, pardon me," he murmured, as he squeezed between two elderly men sitting on the bench. He got up on the bench and stood on his hind legs. Charles peered through the bars on the window. He could see outside, down into the prison's large courtyard.

Charles's mouth dropped open. A piercing cry escaped from his lips. The guards were dragging prisoners from the building and hacking them to death with swords in the courtyard. The dead, their executioners, and the courtyard itself were drenched in blood.

Charles hit the bars on the window furiously with his front paws once, twice, three times. He sank down to the bench—and from there to the floor.

"What did you see?" a young man whispered. When Charles didn't answer, he asked again. "Please—I want to know. I want to prepare myself."

Charles was shaking all over. He struggled to speak. "Massacre! Bloodbath! So many dead! The guards aren't even waiting to take the condemned prisoners to the guillotine. They're hacking them to pieces in the courtyard."

The young man stared straight ahead. When the jury called out the next name, he stood and walked to the table. A few moments later, the cry went up. "Condemned!"

A woman knelt next to Charles. "It's not happening just here," she whispered.

Charles looked at her without understanding.

She leaned closer to him. "They're murdering prisoners like us in all the prisons of Paris!"

"Charles Evrémonde!" a sharp voice called out.

Charles's heart beat at a furious pace. He walked toward the jury's table. He concentrated on keeping his head high and his muzzle pointing forward. When he reached the table, he forced himself to look straight at Madame Defarge. She looked back at him with complete calm.

A man sitting in the middle of the jury studied the big book of names. "You're living in England now?" he asked without glancing up.

Charles answered, "Yes, but—"

"You've been away from France for twelve years?"

"Yes, but—"

"Evrémonde is an emigrant who has returned to France."

"Condemned!" the jury shouted together as a single voice. Madame Defarge nodded and kept knitting.

Two burly guards seized Charles by the collar of his shirt and started to drag him to the door.

Charles struggled against them—not for his doomed life, but for his dignity. "I can walk on my own four legs!"

One guard kicked him in the ribs. "Give me a minute, and I'll make sure you have *no* legs!"

"Stop! In the name of what I suffered as a prisoner in the Bastille—stop!"

Both jury and guards started shouting. Charles looked up from where he was being dragged. His heart stood still. He blinked hard, afraid that his shocked mind was playing tricks on him.

"Dr. Manette!" he cried.

Dr. Manette crossed the room in long strides. His eyes blazed. His tall figure, white hair, outstretched arm, and pointing finger demanded silence. The noise died down.

The doctor stood in front of the citizen jury. "I am Dr. Alexandre Manette. I was imprisoned in the Bastille for eighteen years in secret, and without a trial."

A murmur swept through the room. "The Bastille! Eighteen years!"

The doctor pointed to Charles. "That prisoner is my son-in-law. He is the beloved husband of my daughter, my only child. He is the father of my grandchild. You, citizens, are victims of the old and terrible oppression. Do not destroy what is dearest to a former victim of the Bastille. Do not reproduce the same terrible cruelty you suffered!"

After a moment of silence, the guards and jury began to shout again.

"The doctor is a famous hero of the revolution!"

"*Vive* Dr. Manette! Long live Dr. Manette!"

"Honor to the prisoner of the Bastille!"

"Save the doctor's son-in-law!"

The citizen holding the big book of names jumped up. "I say we must free Evrémonde! What does the rest of the jury say?"

Jury members and guards shouted, "Free Evrémonde! *Vive* Dr. Manette!" The men holding Charles let him go. A great cheer went up. Charles raised one paw to step toward the doctor.

"Wait!"

Everyone turned in the direction of the commanding voice. Madame Defarge stood up.

"Yes, withdraw today's sentence for Evrémonde," she said. "But let him remain here under the protection of the revolution. As an aristocrat and emigrant, his case must be heard in a formal trial. If he is granted freedom, so be it. The revolution will have spoken."

A new shout went up. "Listen to Citizen Defarge! She is right! *Vive* Citizen Defarge! *Vive* Dr. Manette!"

Charles lowered his paw to the floor. His head was spinning. Condemned to death one moment, granted freedom the next, and now prison! The muscles of his muzzle ached from extreme tension. His side ached from the brutal kick. His eyes turned to Dr. Manette, who began to speak again.

"Citizens! *Merci*, thank you for your support. But please let me argue for Charles Evrémonde's freedom. He is—"

New shouts, new names, new condemnations drowned out the doctor's voice. The jury had moved on to other prisoners.

Dr. Manette gave up the effort and hurried over to Charles. Charles stood on his hind legs and hugged his father-in-law. The familiar scent of a loved one brought tears to Charles's eyes. "You saved my life!"

The doctor hugged Charles's shoulders. "Quick!" he whispered. "We must find a place to talk before they take you back to your cell."

Charles and Dr. Manette retreated to a corner. The doctor knelt so he could whisper directly into Charles's ear.

"Listen carefully. Lucie is in Paris with me—and so are Lizzie and Miss Pross."

A low cry escaped from Charles's throat.

"Shh!" the doctor whispered. "When Lucie received

the letter you sent before you left London, we decided to follow you to Paris. I knew you faced terrible danger here as an Evrémonde. I also knew I would have some power here as a former prisoner of the Bastille. Charles, I believe that I can save you!"

Charles watched the doctor's eyes blaze as he continued to speak.

"For the first time, I can see that my eighteen years of suffering had a purpose. I can save my daughter's loved one. I *will* save you!"

One of the guards called out, "Evrémonde, back to your cell."

Dr. Manette spoke as fast as he could. "I will stay here in La Force as long as the bloodbath continues. I must make sure the mob does not turn against you. Then I will work to get you a speedy trial."

The guard reached them.

Charles whispered, "Tell Lucie and Lizzie my heart is always with them. Tell them to be strong. *Au revoir*, Doctor! Good-bye. Until we meet again!"

The guard led Charles back to his cell.

For four days and four nights, the wild behavior of the mob went on. Blood flowed in the courtyards of all the Paris prisons. Dr. Manette remained in the prison to use his skills to comfort the condemned and to treat anyone who was wounded by mistake. He helped the sick. He took care of everyone—prisoners, guards, old, young, aristocrats, and servants. His reputation as a healer and as a hero of the Bastille spread throughout Paris.

After four days, the crazed actions of the mob died down. The uncontrolled crowds had spilled the blood of more than eleven hundred prisoners. Charles remained in his cell. When the killing stopped, Dr. Manette visited him.

"Charles," the doctor said, "my influence in Paris has grown. Now I will use it to get you a fair trial. I located Monsieur Gabelle, the administrator of your lands. He's alive, thank goodness, although weak. He leaves prison today and will testify on your behalf whenever your trial takes place."

Charles clasped Dr. Manette's hands in his front paws. He marveled at how strong and confident the doctor looked after four such terrible days. He had no doubt that the doctor would help him.

When Charles awakened the next morning, he scratched another line on the wall with the pebble. "Two weeks in La Force," he murmured. "Just a few more days, and I will be free, and back with my loved ones!"

But it wasn't a few more days—or a few more weeks— or a few more months. A year went by. Then one . . . two . . . three more months. By December 1793, Charles had scratched more than four hundred fifty lines on the walls of his cell. He had paced enough miles to cover the distance between Paris and London many times—but he had gone nowhere.

Dr. Manette, who was appointed physician for all the prisons in Paris, visited Charles every week. The loving messages he brought from Lucie and Lizzie gave Charles strength. The doctor also convinced one guard to let Charles walk occasionally along a long upper corridor in the afternoon for exercise. Charles noticed a barred window there. It looked down on the dark, dirty corner of a small, winding street.

"Dr. Manette!" Charles said the next time the doctor visited him in his cell. "I think I've found a way to see Lucie and Lizzie! At least for a precious second or two. If they stand on the corner, and if the guard isn't watching for a moment, I can look out the window and see them in the street below."

Charles's whiskers were quivering with emotion. He grasped Dr. Manette's hands with trembling paws.

"They won't be able to see me. And I can't predict which afternoons I'll be allowed into the corridor. But what joy to behold them just once!"

That evening Dr. Manette told Lucie about the window. The next day he showed her where to stand on the corner of the little, winding street. And stand there she did—in the rain and sleet of winter, in the chilling winds of spring and fall, and in the blazing sun of summer. When the weather was good, Lucie brought Lizzie along with her. But even on the worst days, she never considered staying home herself. Like a guardian of love, she arrived at her post every afternoon at two o'clock. She remained there until four o'clock, always gazing up at the barred window.

"You must never gesture toward the prison window or try to communicate in any way," Dr. Manette cautioned his daughter. "The law forbids it. Someone could accuse you of being a spy."

So Lucie stood perfectly still on her corner every day for well over a year. Only silent messages of love came from her lips. Inside the prison, Charles could never predict when the guard would allow him into the corridor. When he finally got there, he could step up to the window only if the guard dozed off or was distracted. For every five or six times Lucie stood outside, Charles saw her only once. Yet the two of them would have continued their efforts to have that tiny bit of companionship—even if they succeeded only once in four hundred times.

Dr. Manette brought Charles news of the revolution— news that horrified him. An extended period of terror had begun. King Louis had lost his head to the guillotine. So had his queen, Marie Antoinette. The prisons were filled to bursting with people from every level of society—all accused of being enemies of the revolution. The guillotine never paused in its deadly work. Every day, large, open farm carts called tumbrils rolled through the streets. They carried the condemned to the guillotine. Charles could hear the heavy wheels as they rumbled past La Force. The sound filled him with despair— for himself and for France.

One gray morning that December, Charles heard footsteps in the passageway outside his cell. *It must be Dr. Manette*, he thought.

The key clinked in the lock. A guard opened the door, and Dr. Manette walked in. He took one of Charles's paws and squeezed it. His eyes looked even more intense than usual.

"Tomorrow, Charles," the doctor said, "your trial will begin!"

Chapter Fourteen

Armed guards took Charles and four other prisoners from La Force prison to the court building. They sat in the hallway outside the courtroom. The stone bench felt icy against his fur. He shivered with tension. His case would be presented next. The Revolutionary Tribunal had already tried and condemned fifteen prisoners that morning.

Fifteen condemned to death in less than an hour and a half! Charles thought. *Why should this tribunal spare me?*

"Charles Evrémonde, also called Charles Darnay!" a stern voice announced.

As Charles walked into the courtroom, his dark brown eyes searched frantically for the blue ones he had not seen for so long. He found them.

Lucie! My darling! Charles's heart pounded. His lips and whiskers trembled. Tears came to his eyes when Lucie leaned forward on the bench where she sat. The expression on her lovely face spoke ever so clearly to him. *Be strong*, it said. *I am with you!*

Charles saw Dr. Manette, Jarvis Lorry, and Monsieur Gabelle sitting on the same bench as Lucie. He nodded his head in their direction. Then he turned to face the

115

Revolutionary Tribunal. The day before, Dr. Manette had described to him how the trial would proceed. The public prosecutor would accuse Charles. The president would question him. The jury would decide his fate. Dr. Manette had given Charles exact instructions on how to answer every possible question that might be asked during his trial.

Charles's eyes opened wide with surprise when he looked at the jury. They were eating, laughing, talking, and even singing. A few appeared quite drunk; a few were sleeping. Charles could smell wine, beer, and stronger liquors in the stale air. More noise—cheering, shouting, loud snoring— came from the crowded visitors' balcony. Only one observer sat silent and calm. Charles was not surprised to see her there. Madame Defarge sat in the front row. She stared straight ahead. Her knitting needles moved back and forth, back and forth . . .

Charles quieted every muscle and every nerve in his body—from those around his ears to those in the tip of his tail. He had to focus all of his energy on the trial. One mistaken word, one misplaced gesture, and he would ride in a tumbril to the guillotine.

The public prosecutor rose. "Charles Evrémonde, also called Charles Darnay, is an emigrant. He is condemned under the law that forbids emigrants to return to France on the penalty of death."

One juror jumped up. "Take off his head!"

"To the guillotine!" several others shouted.

The president rang a bell to call for order. When the shouting died down, he questioned Charles. "Isn't it a simple fact that you lived in England for many years and then returned to France?"

Charles steadied his voice as he began to speak. "I am not an emigrant in the true meaning of the law. I left France long ago in order to be rid of the title of 'marquis,' which I did not want. I rejected the life of an aristocrat. I went to England to earn my own living. I refused to live off the poor peasants of France."

"Didn't you get married in England?"

"I married the French-born daughter of a French citizen—Dr. Alexandre Manette."

A cheer rose from the crowd—just as Dr. Manette had predicted it would.

"*Vive* Dr. Manette! *Vive* the hero of the Bastille!"

Charles's tail wagged ever so slightly. *So far, so good.*

The president of the tribunal glanced at his papers and then looked at Dr. Manette. "The doctor may speak to the tribunal as a witness."

Dr. Manette stood up. His strong, dignified manner calmed the crowd. He spoke with precision and feeling. "When I arrived in England after eighteen years in the Bastille, Charles Evrémonde was my first and dearest French friend."

Dr. Manette described Charles's life in England as a teacher, husband, and father. Then he explained Charles's return to France.

"He came back for one reason—to help a friend in need. That friend sits in this court today as a witness. He is Monsieur Théophile Gabelle."

Monsieur Gabelle started to rise, but a great uproar in the visitors' balcony stopped him.

"Free Evrémonde!"

"*Vive* Dr. Manette's son-in-law!"

Charles's heart beat faster.

One juror shouted, "We've heard enough! Free the prisoner! Let justice be done!"

Several dozen people rushed down from the visitors' balcony and surrounded Charles. He saw new emotions on their faces—generosity, mercy, affection. Tears of joy ran down many cheeks.

"Vive Evrémonde! Vive la révolution! Vive la France!"

A huge cheering citizen lifted Charles onto his shoulders and began a wild dance. As he whirled, the courtroom spun in front of Charles's eyes. The shouting and singing rang in his ears. He searched for Lucie and finally caught sight of her pale, upturned face. He stretched out his front paws toward her. "Let me down! Please! I want to be with my wife!"

The noise of the celebration drowned out his voice. The faces in the wild crowd looked just as menacing as ever to Charles.

They've lost all good sense, he thought. *They could just as well be tearing me to pieces!*

"Stop! In the name of the revolution, I say stop!"

A single voice broke through the uproar. Charles's heart skipped a beat. In an instant, his four paws and nose turned icy. He knew that voice. He twisted his head around to look at the visitors' balcony. Madame Defarge stood on a bench, both arms raised high. In one hand, she held her knitting. In the other, she clutched some folded papers.

"Stop!"

The president rang his bell. Like one immense creature, the mob turned toward the sound of the voice and bell. The noise died down.

"I have other accusations against the prisoner Evré-monde!" Madame Defarge exclaimed. She waved the papers in her hand.

"Who accuses him?" the president asked.

"Two people," Madame Defarge answered. She hurried down from the balcony and stood at the front of the courtroom. "The first—*c'est moi!* It is I, Madame Defarge!"

"And who is the second?" the president asked.

Madame Defarge's eyes flashed as they swept over the entire courtroom. She held the folded paper even higher and called out, "Dr. Alexandre Manette!"

Chapter Fifteen

Madame Defarge's words plunged the courtroom into a strange, almost supernatural, silence. A moment later, the rowdy shouting and shoving began all over again. The president rang his bell once, twice, three times.

Charles jumped down from the dancing man's shoulders to the floor. But before he could take a step in any direction, two guards grabbed him by his coat. They pulled him back to the prisoner's stand. He strained to find Lucie in the crowd. He finally saw her, white as a sheet, leaning on Jarvis Lorry's shoulder. Dr. Manette stood next to them, his fists clenched, his face flushed with anger. As soon as the level of noise dropped, he spoke.

"Honored President, I protest! This accusation is a lie! I demand to know who is behind it. I would never speak out against Charles Evrémonde. How could I? My daughter and those who are dear to her are more precious to me than my own life!"

The president rang his bell to silence the doctor. "Citizen Manette, if you interrupt the proceedings of this tribunal again, I will have you arrested. As for what's precious to you—the revolution must be the most precious of all! If the revolution asks you to sacrifice your only daughter, you must do so gladly!"

A great cheer went up from the crowd in the courtroom. *"Vive la révolution!"*

Dr. Manette said nothing else, but he remained standing. His eyes—and those of everyone else in the room—turned to Madame Defarge.

"Citizen Defarge, can you prove this accusation?" the president asked.

Madame Defarge nodded. For once, her knitting needles didn't move. She spoke calmly. She fixed a steady gaze on Charles. With every word, Charles felt himself moving closer to the guillotine.

"I was among the citizens who stormed the Bastille on July 14, 1789. When the prison was taken over by us, I examined the cell where Dr. Manette once spent eighteen years. I found this letter hidden behind a loose stone in the chimney. The letter is signed by the doctor."

Madame Defarge gave the folded papers to the president. He looked at them briefly, then handed them to an officer of the tribunal. The officer walked over to Dr. Manette to show him the letter.

The doctor shrank back, as if the letter were a deadly poison. "Yes, it's mine!" he cried. "Don't come any closer!"

"Read the letter aloud," the president said to the officer.

As the officer began to read, all eyes in the courtroom shifted to Dr. Manette. He stood as motionless as a stone, listening.

"I, Dr. Alexandre Manette, write this letter on December 31, 1772. I have spent the last ten years in a cell here in the Bastille. My mind is still sound, and what I am about to write is true and correct. I must write

quickly because I'm often spied upon. I pray that someone will find this letter someday and know my terrible story. By then, my mind will be long gone, and my body will be dust.

"Exactly ten years ago, I was traveling from the city of Rouen to my home in Paris. I stopped for the night at a small country inn where I had stayed before and was known. In the middle of the night, the innkeeper awakened me. He said a doctor was needed immediately, and in great secret.

"I was taken to an isolated farmhouse, where I found a young woman about twenty years old, and her brother, who was sixteen. The young woman, alas, was already dead. She had drowned. The boy suffered from a deep sword wound to the chest. I made the boy as comfortable as I could, but I knew he would not survive the night. With his last bit of strength, he told me what had happened.

"His family lived as peasants on land belonging to the Marquis Saint Evrémonde. Both his father and mother had died the previous year from doing too much work and having too little food. That very afternoon, his sister had been kidnapped by the marquis's younger brother—an Evrémonde even more wicked than the cruel marquis. The sister escaped her captor by throwing herself into the river, where she drowned. The boy tracked down the criminal aristocrat and attacked him with a knife.

"Everyone knows that a French aristocrat damages his honor if he 'soils' his sword with the blood of a peasant. But this peasant boy fought so fiercely that he forced Evrémonde to draw his sword and defend himself. Evrémonde pierced the boy's chest and drew blood. If anyone finds this out, the family name will be *shamed. The poor boy smiled at this thought and died in my arms.*

"I returned to the inn, where the innkeeper revealed yet another secret. One member of the peasant family— a younger sister—was still alive. Neighbors had rushed her to relatives far away. They wanted to protect her from the wrath of the Marquis Saint Evrémonde and his brother.

"These terrible events weighed on my mind and heart when I returned to Paris the next day. I held my beloved young wife and our baby daughter, Lucie, close to my heart for hours. I decided I must write to a government official and speak out against the crimes of the marquis's brother. I mailed the letter on the following morning.

"Late the next night, I was walking home after seeing a patient. An armed man stopped me on an empty street and forced me into a carriage. Two other men stepped out of the shadows. They glanced at me, nodded to the coachman, and the carriage drove off. It brought me straight to the Bastille—to this horrible stone grave of the living dead.

"The instant I saw those two men step out of the shadows, I knew their names as surely as I know my own. They dressed like aristocrats of high rank. They resembled each other so closely that I knew they were brothers. One had a coat of arms and the letter 'E' embroidered on his waistcoat. They were the Marquis Saint Evrémonde and his younger brother. They had certainly been told about my letter speaking out against them. They had decided to punish me by ending my life among the living.

"For ten years, neither brother has allowed me a word of news about my precious wife and daughter. These brothers are monsters without a trace of human feeling. They have pierced my heart, just as they pierced the heart

of that young peasant boy. They are tormenting me to death, just as they tormented the peasants on their land.

I, Alexandre Manette, call out to heaven and to earth and charge them with all their crimes. I charge them and their descendants down to the very last of the Evrémonde family."

Charles was trembling so violently that his white fur shimmered. He couldn't take his eyes off Dr. Manette. *Who condemned you to the Bastille? My father, the marquis; and my uncle, his younger brother, who would be the future marquis. That was your secret! And still you took me into your family!* Two tears moistened the sides of his muzzle.

The doctor slowly turned his head toward Charles. He mouthed the words, *Forgive me.*

The president rang his bell to quiet the crowd. "The tribunal must still hear from Citizen Defarge," he said. "The citizen will explain why she has accused Charles Evrémonde."

Madame Defarge rose from her seat. Once again, she looked at Charles as she spoke. "I accuse all Evrémondes, including this one, because I am the sister of that boy with the pierced heart! I am the sister of that young woman who drowned herself!"

With one hand, she pointed a knitting needle at Charles. With the other hand, she held up the long scarf she was knitting.

"Do you know what is being knitted in this scarf?" she asked. "A list of those who must die. I began knitting it many years ago in a secret code. And do you know what is the first name on the list? Evrémonde! In the name of the revolution, I demand justice!"

"To the guillotine!"

"Take off his head!"

The president rang his bell and began to ask the jury members, one by one, to declare a verdict.

"Condemned!"

"Condemned!"

"Condemned!"

Charles stopped listening. He and Lucie looked at each other. He stretched out a paw as far as he could—as if trying to reach across the room to touch her. She stretched out both hands. Tears streamed down her cheeks. She sobbed so hard that her shoulders shook.

A man wearing a red cap entered the courtroom and announced the start of a public procession outside. The president quickly dismissed the tribunal for the day. The crowd began to rush out of the room. The citizens now had other matters on their minds. Not one—except Madame Defarge—even looked at Charles while hurrying to the door.

"Please, kind citizens, have pity on me," Lucie pleaded to the guards and soldiers who remained in the courtroom. "Let me touch my husband one last time!"

The two guards near Charles hesitated, then nodded. Lucie rushed forward. Charles, still on the prisoner's stand, stood on his hind legs and stretched out his front paws. The couple embraced. Lucie wrapped her arms around Charles's neck. As she buried her face in his soft fur, Charles breathed in her delicate scent. He had missed that smell more than any other in the world. Lucie laid her smooth, pale cheek against his muzzle and lifted her blue eyes to his brown ones.

"Farewell, darling of my heart," Charles said softly. "We shall meet again in heaven."

"We will, Charles!" Lucie replied. "I know that, and so I am given the strength to go on. Now give me a parting word to take to our daughter."

"I say farewell and give her my love through you," Charles said.

Tears fell from Lucie's eyes.

One of the guards moved toward Charles.

"No, wait!" Lucie cried. "Dear husband, we won't be separated for long. I know my heart will break from this ordeal. I will care for Lizzie and my father until I join you. Then our dear friends will care for the two of them. You—"

The guard seized one sleeve of Charles's coat. Dr. Manette lurched toward them and sank to his knees. Jarvis Lorry immediately tried to get his friend to stand up, but the doctor shook Lorry off and let loose a horrible cry. The guard began to pull Charles toward the door. Charles kept one paw stretched out toward Lucie, and his eyes remained fixed on hers.

It could not have turned out differently, Charles thought. *Good could never have come from the Evrémonde evil. A happy end could never have come from such unhappiness.*

Charles passed through the doorway. A guard slammed the door shut behind him. As soon as Lucie could no longer see Charles, her eyelids fluttered and began to close. She swayed. Jarvis Lorry, trying to calm Dr. Manette, didn't notice. Lucie sank, her full skirt billowing out farther.

Before her head hit the floor, a pair of steady arms caught her, cradled her slim figure, and lifted her up gently. She remained in a deep faint, but safe. A dark head bent over her golden curls and whispered, "I will never let you fall, Lucie. Never."

Sydney Carton carried Lucie to the nearest bench and sat down with her. He supported her head and shoulders. Jarvis Lorry followed them, leading Dr. Manette. The doctor's head hung down. His eyes were wide open, but he saw nothing.

"Mr. Lorry," Sydney said in a low voice, "listen to me carefully. The lives of Lucie, Lizzie, and maybe Dr. Manette depend completely on what I'm about to say to you."

126

"Good heavens, Carton! What are you doing here?" Jarvis Lorry exclaimed.

"Shh!" Sydney glanced around. "There's no time to lose. I've been in Paris for several days, finding out everything I could. Lucie and Lizzie are in very serious danger. That Defarge woman wants to send Evrémonde's wife and daughter to the guillotine. She's going to accuse them of passing messages to foreign spies. I have a plan—it's the only chance to save them. Will you promise—on your love for them—to do exactly what I say?"

Jarvis Lorry's eyes opened wider and wider. He had never seen Sydney Carton so passionate, so focused, and so completely without bitterness. "Yes, I promise! On my love for them!"

Holding Lucie with perfect gentleness, Sydney spoke to Jarvis Lorry in a calm and clear voice. "You and Miss Pross must pack up the household tonight. Arrange for a hired coach to travel to Calais tomorrow. Have the coach pick you up in the courtyard of Tellson's bank. There's less chance of someone noticing you there. By two o'clock tomorrow afternoon, you all must be sitting in the coach, ready to leave—that means you, Lucie, Dr. Manette, Lizzie, and Miss Pross. The remaining seat is for me. The moment I am in my seat, the coach must depart."

Jarvis Lorry nodded. "It will be done exactly as you say."

Sydney handed him a folded document. "This is my passport to leave France. Hold it for me until tomorrow. Be sure all the others have their passports."

Sydney's voice became fierce after a moment.

"The execution will take place at three o'clock. No matter what happens, the carriage must leave as soon as you take me in. Wait for no one else! Let nothing delay the departure. And in the name of all that's still good in the world, go quickly—to Calais, to the ferry boat, and back to England."

"I am an old man," Jarvis Lorry said, "but your passion inspires me. I can—and will—do it!"

"And now," Sydney said, "we'll find a carriage so you can take Lucie to her apartment. Somehow, she and Lizzie must get through this terrible night."

Sidney carried Lucie out of the courthouse as if she were a priceless package that weighed no more than a feather. Jarvis Lorry found them a carriage and got in first. Sydney lifted Lucie onto the seat, arranged her head on a pillow, then kissed her forehead.

As he raised his head, he murmured, "Do you remember what I said the day you returned from your wedding trip? I would give my life to keep a life you love beside you. I know you remember."

Sydney watched the carriage move up the busy street until it passed out of view. He touched his fingers to his lips, sending Lucie one last sign of devotion. Then he turned away. He glanced at his pocket watch and hurried around the corner to a side entrance of the courthouse. He waited by the door until a man wearing an English-style coat approached. The man had cool gray eyes and an unpleasant manner. His black hair was just starting to turn gray.

"There he is," Sydney muttered to himself. "John Barsad. Aside from the gray streaks in his hair, he looks just the same as he did thirteen years ago, in 1780. I can still picture him at the Old Bailey courthouse in London, accusing Charles of spying. I can still picture him tumbling head over heels that time I kicked him down the stairs when he cheated at dice."

When John Barsad reached him, Sydney spoke aloud.

"I see that you received the message I sent this morning. And you've arrived exactly on time for the meeting I proposed."

Barsad glared at Sydney with a mixture of fear and hatred. "We can't talk here," he said in a hushed voice. "Let's walk down the street."

The two men began to walk in the direction of the Notre Dame cathedral. Barsad's eyes darted to the left and right. He clenched and unclenched his fists. Sydney Carton walked casually, his hands in his pockets. He whistled an old English tune.

"Stop that whistling!" Barsad hissed. "Do you want everyone to notice us?"

"Sorry," Sydney said. "I forgot how much you always have to hide. I hear you're working as a prison spy for the current French government. When we last met—at the Old Bailey, you were working for the Marquis Saint Evrémonde—"

"Shh!" Barsad glanced around. "Don't you know that's enough to get me sent to the guillotine?"

"I know that quite well," Sydney said. He sighed. "I'm

afraid I'm going to use that information to encourage you to do me a favor. Considering what your current job is, I assume you can get in and out of the prisons easily."

"I can," Barsad whispered. "But don't think that means I'd help your friend Charles escape. Other people have tried to escape from these French prisons. It's impossible."

"Believe me—I have no plans of setting up an escape," Sydney said. "I know that no one can get Charles out of this disastrous situation. You'll be doing something else for me—"

Barsad's face flushed. "What makes you think I'll do what you want?"

"Because," Sydney replied in a matter-of-fact voice, "you must. If not, I will go directly to the Revolutionary Tribunal and tell them about you and the marquis."

Barsad gritted his teeth and said nothing.

Sydney took Barsad by the arm. "Now, listen very carefully. . . ."

In the middle of the worst possible crisis, Sydney Carton has a plan. I love that kind of courage and inventiveness. But some desperate situations leave even the best of us stumped.

For example, take the baby-sitting disaster back in Oakdale. I have a full-scale uprising—involving two five-year-old girls and unraveling toilet paper—on my paws. I can't do anything but wait for help to arrive.

Chapter Sixteen

Wishbone lay flat on his stomach, under a chair in the living room. He covered his head with his front paws. "Air assault under way. Missiles coming in from all directions. Commando Wishbone has taken cover."

Emily and Tina were dancing around the living room and hallway with their rolls of toilet paper. They draped yards of it over the furniture. They ran paper trails along the floor. They hung streamers from the staircase bannister. The rooms looked like a jungle—a white-toilet-paper jungle.

"You guys are in trouble," Wishbone muttered. "*Big* trouble! Commando Wishbone may be in temporary retreat, but other members of his special Oakdale citizens' unit are on the way. I mean—Joe and Ellen have to come home sometime, right?"

The girls were laughing, squealing, and shouting, but Wishbone picked up a new sound. A key turned in the front-door lock. The door opened, and Ellen called out, "Joe, I'm home." Emily and Tina glanced at each other, then scooted behind the far end of the couch.

Wishbone jumped out from under the chair. "Ellen!

Great! Reinforcements have arrived! Together we can end this madness."

Ellen took a few steps into the hallway, then stopped abruptly. She looked confused, then horrified. Wishbone ran over to meet her, his tail waving like an army battalion flag.

"I know it's bad, Ellen. But together we can flush out the enemy, disarm them, then take them into custody. We can accuse them of crimes committed against the household and put them on trial. We can—"

Ellen took a few more steps, then slowly turned to look at Wishbone. "How could you go and make such a mess?" she asked.

Wishbone's tail stopped moving. "*Me?* Commando Wishbone? No, you don't understand. I'm on *your* side. I'll show you who did it." He trotted toward the couch. "We'll surprise them in their hideout."

Ellen followed Wishbone to the far side of the couch. Tina and Emily were sitting on the floor, quietly drawing pictures. They had arranged Emily's crayons and paper in neat piles. They looked up at Ellen and smiled sweetly.

Wishbone barked. "Don't be fooled by the nice-little-girl disguises. It's the oldest terrorist trick in the book."

Ellen looked even more confused. "Emily! What are you doing here?"

"David and Joe are baby-sitting for us," Emily said. "This is Tina."

"Can you tell me what's going on in this house?" Ellen asked.

Wishbone nudged Ellen's leg with his shoulder. "Don't ask them! They'll give you misinformation. They'll lead you into a trap or an ambush."

When Emily didn't answer, Ellen said, "I guess the boys are outside. I'd better go find them."

Five minutes later, Joe, David, Emily, and Tina were sitting in a row on the couch. Wishbone hopped onto a nearby armchair. Ellen paced back and forth in front of the couch.

Wishbone nodded his approval. "A trial, fair and square. Air all the facts. Rely on expert testimony—from me. Call witnesses—me. And prove who's guilty—*them*." He picked up an empty cardboard toilet-paper spool with his teeth and dropped it on the floor. "Evidence—exhibit A."

"Okay, somebody talk to me," Ellen said. "What's the story here?"

Wishbone barked. "I swear to tell the truth, the whole truth, and nothing but the—"

"Quiet, Wishbone," Ellen said. She looked at Joe and David.

Wishbone lay down. "Need I say it? *Nobody ever listens to the dog.*"

David cleared his throat nervously. "I was supposed to baby-sit, but I wanted to test out my remote-control car with Joe."

Joe nodded. "That's right. And I was sort of helping David to baby-sit."

Wishbone lifted his head. "So far, so good. I can confirm all of this."

"Right," David said, "and the girls—they didn't want to go outside with us."

"No," Emily said, "they didn't want us!"

Ellen looked at Joe. "Well, you guys should have stayed where you could keep an eye on the girls. I mean—it's a good thing they're so well behaved."

Wishbone sat up. "Objection, Your Honor!"

Ellen went on. "Joe, Wishbone has made a total mess. He's in big trouble. I want you to put him out on the back porch—now."

Wishbone sprang up on all fours. "Hey! What kind of trial is this? You can't just sentence me. Where's your evidence? What about witnesses? And when do I get to testify?"

Joe sighed and moved toward Wishbone. "Sorry, boy," he said softly.

Wishbone jumped off the chair. "I demand justice! This is the United States of America!"

Joe grabbed Wishbone's collar and started to pull him toward the kitchen.

Wishbone barked. "Wait a minute! What happened to liberty and justice for all?"

Just look at me—falsely accused, then sentenced without a fair trial. How can I not think of poor Charles Darnay in Paris? I'm condemned to the back porch— which is bad enough. Poor Charles, however, is going to the guillotine!

Chapter Seventeen

Charles walked up and down the length of his prison cell with nervous steps. The light had faded, but his pace had not slowed. Try as he might, he couldn't get control of his thoughts. His mind was moving even faster than his four legs.

This is the end—my last night. I must prepare for death and meet it with calm and some kind of understanding. The image of Lucie's face took shape before his eyes. He stopped pacing. *My love! I want to be with you! I don't want to die!* He saw Lizzie's young face. *My dearest! I want to see you grow up! I want to see your children—my grandchildren!* He moaned and forced the images to fade from his mind.

My hold on life is too strong. He flexed and released the muscles of his four paws several times—as if trying to let go of life. *Why is this so hard?* He began pacing again. Once more, he pictured Lucie and Lizzie. He imagined them after his death. A new thought came to him. *If they know I died with dignity and strength, they will live afterward with greater peace of mind.*

Charles realized this was true. His four legs, mind, and even the beating of his heart slowed down. His whiskers

135

stopped quivering. Another thought came to him. *If I find inner strength tonight, I can help the other prisoners tomorrow.*

Charles breathed in deeply. He walked to the small table and jumped onto the chair next to it. The guards had allowed him to buy a quill pen, ink, paper, and a small oil lamp. He picked up the pen in his teeth and dipped it into the ink. He wrote three farewell letters. He worded each sentence of each letter carefully. He wanted to soothe and strengthen the readers.

To Lucie, he communicated his eternal love and asked her to care for their daughter. He also asked her to comfort Dr. Manette and convince him not to blame himself for what had happened. She must remind him that he had made their life together possible.

To Dr. Manette, he recalled his respect and affection, and asked him to care for Lucie and Lizzie. Charles hoped that a sense of duty would help to strengthen the doctor's health.

To Jarvis Lorry, he recalled his deep friendship and asked him to care for all the others. He also wrote down the necessary information about his finances and property.

Charles finished addressing the third letter, then put down his pen. For the last time in his life, he stretched out on the straw mattress. Covering his forehead with his front paws, he continued to worry about how his household would manage without him. His thoughts never strayed to anyone outside the family, not even to Sydney Carton.

Charles hoped for a deep and dreamless sleep. But vivid images of people and places interrupted his rest: the tall, thin man of Saint Antoine holding up his dead child; his uncle, the marquis, dining in the château; Sydney Carton staring at the ceiling in the Old Bailey courtroom; biscuits and tea in the house in Soho; the mob surrounding his horse on the road to Paris; Madame Defarge pointing her knitting needles at—

"The guillotine!" The sound of Charles's own howl awakened him. He sat up, his tongue hanging out of his mouth, panting. The cold night air felt like frost on his sweat-soaked fur.

The dawn was breaking. Charles stood and shook himself hard. He knew he couldn't sleep anymore. He walked around his cell to warm up. A wave of new thoughts swept through his mind.

Exactly what should I expect at three o'clock this afternoon? They say fifty-two prisoners will lose their heads at that hour. But will I be one of the first or the last? How many steps will I climb to reach the platform of the guillotine? Will I be blindfolded or not? Do I position my head myself, or does someone help me? Will the people who touch me have blood on their hands?

Charles gave himself up to this flood of questions for more than an hour. The clock in the prison tower struck nine.

"I will never hear a clock strike that number again," Charles murmured. He noticed a ray of pale winter light shining through the grate far above his head. All the questions he had been asking seemed foolish and unnecessary. He felt a sense of peace settle over his body. It moved down the back of his head, along his spine, and down the length of his tail.

Charles began to walk slowly. Every time he placed a paw on the stone floor, he murmured Lucie's or Lizzie's name. He breathed quietly, easily. The clock struck ten, eleven, twelve. The hours passed neither slowly nor quickly. The clock struck one.

How strange, Charles thought. *I feel like a very different creature from the prisoner who paced back and forth in this cell more than a year ago. I'm ready to die.*

Charles heard two sets of quiet footsteps outside in the passageway. A key turned in the lock of his cell. As the door opened, someone whispered in English, "This is his cell. I'll wait outside. Be quick!"

Charles's heart skipped a beat. His eyes blinked several times in disbelief. Sydney Carton stepped into the cell. He wore a large tan wool coat that reached the floor and had an attached cape. His tall, round hat had a floppy brim and deep blue band.

Sydney smiled and held a finger up to his lips. "I know I'm the last person in the world you expected to see today. But don't say a word—just listen. Everything I'm going to ask you to do is something your dear wife wants with all her heart. So now—change my tie for yours."

Charles remained still—too amazed and puzzled to react. Sydney pulled off his own dark English tie first, then Charles's light-colored one. Before he could utter a word, Charles was wearing Sydney's tie around his furred neck.

Charles finally spoke. "My dear Sydney, this is madness! You can't smuggle me out of here. Others have tried to do so and always failed. Do you want to add your own death to mine?"

Sydney's voice was cheerful. "Did I ever suggest that you would walk out of this cell? No. So don't bother protesting unless I do. Now, sit down at the table. Hurry, my friend! Write what I dictate to you. Hurry!"

Sydney had already pushed Charles toward the table. Charles hopped onto the chair. Sydney thrust the pen and paper toward him and began dictating.

"Write this: 'If you remember the words that passed between us long ago—'"

Charles didn't pick up the pen. He looked around at Sydney, who stood just behind him. "To whom do I address the letter?"

"No one. Just write quickly!"

"Should I date the letter?" Charles asked. He noticed that Sydney kept his right hand tucked inside his coat.

"No date. Just write! 'If you remember the words that

passed between us long ago, you will understand this letter.'"

Charles picked up the pen in his teeth, wrote for a moment, then glanced around. Sydney had started to pull his right hand out from under his coat. He put it back inside as soon as Charles moved.

Charles put down the pen. "You're holding something in your hand. What is it? A weapon?"

"No," Sydney said. "I'm not armed. But for your wife's sake, hurry! Pick up the pen and write: 'I'm thankful the time has come when I can prove them.'"

As Charles wrote, Sydney's hand again moved slowly out of his coat. It held a damp handkerchief. Sydney moved his hand near Charles's muzzle. Charles's head drooped. The pen fell to the table. His head jerked up. Sydney pulled his hand back.

"What . . . what was that?" Charles asked. "A . . . strange smell. I feel faint."

"I didn't smell anything," Sydney whispered. "Write faster—much faster! We've almost finished."

Charles gripped the pen firmly in his teeth and bent his head to finish the sentence. He couldn't remember the words. He couldn't see the page clearly. He had trouble speaking. "You said . . . what?"

Sydney repeated the sentence. "'I'm thankful the time has come when I can prove them.'"

His hand reached around Charles's muzzle again. The sleek white head dropped down. The pen left a trail of ink on the page. Without warning, the head snapped back up. Charles moved his four legs, as if to jump off the chair. With his left arm, Sydney grasped Charles around his belly. With his right hand, he pressed the handkerchief, which was soaked with a sleeping drug, to Charles's moist black nose. The furred body went limp. Charles lay unconscious in Sydney's arms.

Sydney didn't waste an instant. With rapid and exact motions, he moved Charles over to the straw mattress. He pulled off his own heavy tan coat and put it on Charles. He arranged the folds of cloth to look as if they were wrapped around a long, limp body. He took off his tall hat and pulled it over Charles's head and floppy ears. He tucked the unfinished letter into a coat pocket, opened the cell door a crack, and whispered, "You—come in now!"

John Barsad slinked into the cell. His gray eyes were darting right and left. He bit his nails. "You'd better keep your part of the bargain, Carton."

"I will," Sydney replied. "And you'd better start addressing my friend here as 'Sydney Carton.'" He pointed to Charles. "Now, get your men to carry him out. If anyone asks what happened, say Carton was ill to begin with, and that he was then overcome with emotion by saying good-bye to his friend."

Barsad trembled. "You'd better hold up your end in all of this."

Sydney pushed him to the door. "I will obviously be true to the death. So stop wasting time! Just get this fellow safely into the coach waiting at the Paris office of Tellson's bank as fast as you can. Tell Jarvis Lorry to let Carton awaken on his own. It will take at least fifteen hours for the sleeping potion to wear off."

Barsad stepped out into the passageway and returned with two men carrying a stretcher. Sydney and Barsad placed Charles on the stretcher. The men lifted it.

As they carried the stretcher out the cell door, Sydney's fingertips touched Charles one last time. "Bring them all safely back to England," he whispered, "and happily through the rest of this life."

Sydney turned to Barsad. He whispered, "Don't forget to lock the cell."

"I'm happy to shut you in," Barsad muttered as he left.

Sydney smiled. "No, I'm shutting myself in." He closed the door.

Chapter Eighteen

The clock struck the quarter-hour: one-forty-five. Madame Defarge marched through the muddy streets of Paris like a general armed for battle—head high, eyes straight ahead, dagger thrust under her sash, pistol hidden in the front of her dress. She went over her attack plan one last time.

I'll find Evrémonde's wife and child at home right now, mourning his execution. The wife will be so upset that she'll say something against the revolution. The child will certainly comfort the mother. Tonight I'll use that information when I speak against them to the Revolutionary Tribunal. I'll accuse them of spying for foreigners and of being enemies of the revolution. I will have their heads! Her tight lips stretched into a smile of satisfaction.

"Hey, watch out! You'll knock us over!"

Madame Defarge stopped short, but she still bumped into a stretcher being carried by two men. She glared at them and looked down at the figure being carried. "What's this? Strange coat and hat. English-style. What's wrong with him?" she demanded to know.

A third man, whose gray eyes darted back and forth, answered her. He spoke poor French with an English accent. "Sick, and probably drunk, too." Then he grabbed one side of the stretcher and shouted at his companions, "Move along! We've got a job to do."

"Wait!" Madame Defarge said. "Foreigners can be fined for drunken—"

The men didn't stop.

Madame Defarge took a step toward them, paused, then crossed the avenue. She turned down a small street. *I have more important matters to take care of,* she thought. *And I want to finish this little errand in time to get to the guillotine early. I left my knitting on my usual front-row seat to mark my place, but we'll have a bigger crowd than usual today. Many citizens want to see Evrémonde's head roll. But no one more than I!*

She entered the courtyard of an old apartment building and hurried to the front entrance. She smiled with satisfaction again as she marched up the five flights of stairs.

The loyal spies of the revolution told me exactly where the family lives. This will be as easy as . . . chopping off a head with a sharp blade. She noticed the building was empty. *All good citizens have left for the three o'clock performance at the guillotine. We'll have a fine crowd!*

At the top of the stairs, she approached the only door. Finding it unlocked, she opened it and stepped inside silently. She entered into a large sitting room, which had a closed door at the opposite wall. Near the closed door, a woman with wild red hair and a red face—Miss Pross—was putting on a bonnet. At first, Miss Pross didn't notice anyone standing in the room. When she finally turned and saw the intruder, she shrieked.

Madame Defarge and Miss Pross stared at each other. They eyed each other up and down, trying to estimate strength and courage. Each stood her ground—fierce, valiant, and ready for battle.

"Where is the wife of Evrémonde?" Madame Defarge asked in French. "I want to speak with her now."

Miss Pross had refused to learn a word of French. Yet she understood that the woman she faced was Lucie's greatest enemy. She had heard enough descriptions of Madame Defarge to know that much. Madame Defarge knew no English, but she understood that the woman she faced would do anything to protect Evrémonde's wife.

Miss Pross spoke next. "I will never let you know the truth—that my ladybird and the others have already left this apartment, and that I'm here alone to lock up. I'll make you think she's in the other room. The coach will depart without me, but I can take a later one. The longer I hold you here, the better are my ladybird's chances to escape."

Madame Defarge never took her eyes off Miss Pross. "You fool!" she said in French. "You can't hide anything from me. Either Evrémonde's wife is in that other room, or she has fled. And if she's fled, I'll have her followed and brought back. So let me see into that room." Madame Defarge took a step toward the closed door.

Miss Pross clenched her fists and leaned forward. "Oh, no, you don't! I won't let you know that room is empty. You'll never touch that door!"

Madame Defarge stood absolutely still and stared at Miss Pross for more than a minute. Then she lunged for the door. Miss Pross grabbed Madame Defarge by the skirt and wrapped her arms around the big woman's waist. Miss Pross's arms held her enemy like a vise. The Frenchwoman beat her fists against Miss Pross's head and shoulders and clawed at her face. Yet nothing could make Miss Pross let go. The two enemies stumbled around the room together like a pair of wild dancers.

Madame Defarge's hands searched at her own waist for her dagger.

Gasping for breath, Miss Pross said, "You won't ever get that dagger out. I've pinned it under my arm."

Madame Defarge searched at the front of her own dress. Miss Pross saw the pistol. Without thinking, she threw up her arms and struck out at the weapon. There was a blinding flash and a deafening blast . . . followed by complete silence.

Madame Defarge dropped to the floor, dead.

"Oh, help! What have I done?" Miss Pross rushed to the apartment door, screaming. She started running down the stairs to get help. "No, wait! Wait!" she told herself. "If anyone finds out what's happened, my ladybird might not escape! Be quiet, Pross! Quiet!"

Using all her willpower, Miss Pross forced herself to calm down and to return to the apartment. *Get your bonnet and the key*, she told herself. Keeping her eyes turned away from the body on the floor, she got her bonnet and the key. She left the apartment again and locked the door behind her. She quickly put on her bonnet and pulled the veil over her scratched and bleeding face.

Choking back sobs, Miss Pross walked as fast as she could toward Tellson's bank. As she crossed one of the stone bridges over the River Seine, she stepped up to the railing. She dropped the apartment key into the water. She didn't allow herself to run for fear of attracting too much attention.

Oh, I pray the coach has gone ahead without me. Every minute gained keeps my loved ones a little farther from disaster. But what if they're waiting for me? Oh, I must get there as quickly as possible!

Miss Pross glanced at a clock tower in the distance: two-fifteen. She rounded the last corner and saw the coach halfway up the street, driving away. She was afraid to call out or wave. Jarvis Lorry, cautiously peering out the back window of the coach, noticed her. He signaled to the driver to stop. Miss Pross plunged down the street. She reached for Mr. Lorry's outstretched hand. He pulled her into the coach and then signaled to the driver to move on.

Inside the coach, Miss Pross allowed herself to cry. But she soon realized that she couldn't hear her own sobs—or anything else. She looked up and saw Mr. Lorry talking to her. She shook her head slowly and spoke to everyone in the coach. "The gun went off. I saw its flash and heard the terrible blast. But now I know that the terrible blast will be the last sound I'll ever hear on this earth. I am deaf."

"What are we supposed to do when we get to the guillotine? Will they tell us where to stand?"

A soft voice interrupted Sydney's thoughts. He looked at the young woman who had spoken to him. She was thin, almost frail, with wide-spaced green eyes and high cheekbones in a delicate face. She looked into Sydney's eyes sadly.

She's hardly more than a child, he thought. *Lucie was only slightly older when I first saw her.*

They stood side by side in a tumbril, their hands tied in front of them. Their tumbril was the third in a procession of six such farm carts. The slanted sides of the tumbrils were made of crude wooden slats. They had formerly carried mostly manure; now each carried eight or nine condemned prisoners.

The clock struck the quarter-hour: two-forty-five. The tumbrils had traveled only part of the distance between the prison and the guillotine. Hundreds of people crowded into every street along the way. They shouted, sang, cheered. They danced around the tumbrils. Dozens more leaned out of windows and waved colored banners. Sydney heard one name again and again.

"Evrémonde! Where's Evrémonde?"

"Evrémonde's head will roll!"

"Down with all aristocrats like Evrémonde!"

Sydney paid no attention to the shouting. He stood in

a shadow. He kept his head down, letting his long hair fall forward. Then he raised his head just enough to speak with the young woman next to him.

Her green eyes filled with tears. "Will I hear the blade coming down?"

Sydney smiled gently at her. "No, my child. You will hear something wonderfully sweet that comes from within you."

She smiled back at him, but still sadly. "I am a seamstress and an orphan in the world. The tribunal said I plotted against the revolution, but, truly, I didn't. The revolution is supposed to make life better for poor people like myself. So I'm happy to die for it. But I don't understand how the death of a poor seamstress will help the revolution. Can you explain it to me?"

Sydney shook his head. "I've always believed that a revolution itself dies the moment it harms one of the people it was supposed to help."

"You have kind eyes," the seamstress said. "Will you hold my hand until the time comes? If you do, I know I won't be afraid."

Sydney stretched out his fingers and entwined them with the delicate fingers of the young seamstress. He looked into her trusting face. *She will be the last creature on earth who warms and softens my heart*, Sydney thought. *How glad I am that we have found each other. I will be father, mother, brother, and sister to her now. And she will be the same for me. How lucky I feel to have yet another purpose at this moment.*

The seamstress smiled again and whispered, "I know you're not Evrémonde."

Sydney's heart skipped a beat.

She went on in the quietest voice. "I saw him last year in La Force prison. You're dying for him?"

Sydney nodded. "And for his wife and child." He put

his fingers to his lips. "Now, hush, my dear child. Not another word about it."

As the tumbril turned a corner, Sydney glanced up at the streets of Paris. He thought of how he had walked the same streets the previous night after having arranged the details of his plan to save Charles. *How calm and content I felt, and yet vigorous, too. For the first time, life seemed sweet and good because I knew what to do with it.*

The clock struck three. The procession of tumbrils arrived in the huge public square where a statue of the king of France once stood. Thousands of shouting spectators had already crowded into the square. Hundreds of them immediately swarmed around the tumbrils, slowing down their progress. The tumbrils finally arrived at the platform on which the guillotine stood. Immediately in front of it were rows of chairs and benches. Several hundred spectators could sit. The rest would stand. A half-dozen steep stairs led up to the platform.

Some prisoners climbed down from the tumbrils themselves. The guards handed the others down. While Sydney waited for the seamstress, he looked at the crowd. *Every seat filled for today's performance*, he thought. *Ah, not quite.* In the first row, he noticed one empty chair on which a knitting basket sat.

Sydney turned away and spoke softly to the seamstress. "Stand over here, facing me." He wanted to make sure that her back was turned to the dreadful guillotine. "Remember to keep your eyes on me. Don't pay attention to anything else."

"Will you tell me when it's time?" she asked.

"Yes."

The fifty-two prisoners condemned to die that day stood close to the platform. The guards had already given each one a number. The seamstress was number twenty-two. Sydney was number twenty-three.

The first prisoner walked up the stairs. The heavy blade was pulled up, then immediately dropped. *Crash!* The crowd cheered and counted. One.

I must distract her from the horrible sounds, Sydney thought. He bent down. "Tell me about yourself, my dear child. Where were you born, and who raised you? Tell me some of your sweetest memories."

The seamstress answered his questions about her short life. When she finished, she added, "You've been such a comfort to me, like a brother."

"And you to me, dear sister," Sydney replied.

"Is it time now?" she asked.

"Yes, my child."

Sydney kissed her forehead. She laid her cheek against his. She turned and climbed the steps up to the platform. The blade rose, then fell. *Crash!* Twenty-two.

It was "Evrémonde's" turn. Several thousand standing spectators surged forward like a human wave. Those who had sat on chairs stood on them to get a better view. The noise of cheering and shouting grew louder.

Sydney walked up the steps, unaware of the crowd. He was thinking of the future. He knew with absolute certainty that what he saw in his mind would come to pass.

I see the lives for which I lay down my own life. They are peaceful, useful, and happy. Lucie and Charles have a new baby. They name him Sydney. Dr. Manette has grown older, but he is healthy and healing others. Jarvis Lorry lives for ten more years, always the loyal friend and advisor.

I see that I hold the most honored place in all their hearts—and in the hearts of their children and their children's children. I see Charles and Lucie, both elderly, weeping for me on the anniversary of this day.

I see their child Sydney grown into a man and following my own profession. He becomes the most honored of wise and fair judges. I see him as a father, too. His son is named Sydney, and he has the golden hair and pale forehead I know so well.

I see these two, father and son, standing on this very place in Paris. But the square has been washed clean. I see a beautiful city and people rising finally from these terrible depths. I see that their struggles to be truly free will someday triumph.

Sydney felt a deep sense of peace moving him forward and lifting him up.

"It is a far, far better thing that I do than I have ever done," Sydney said. "It is a far, far better rest that I go to than I have ever known."

Charles Darnay tried to move, but his body felt strangely heavy. He tried to speak, but his entire muzzle felt frozen. He heard sounds, but they were fuzzy and distant.

Where am I? In my prison cell . . . with Sydney. Carton, dear friend, I tell you that escape is impossible!

Charles's nose picked up a lovely scent—a familiar scent. *Lucie!* Tears moistened his closed eyes. *My mind is playing cruel tricks on me.* His ears picked up a familiar sound—Lucie's voice.

"I think he's finally awakening! Yes, I'm sure of it!"

Charles's eyelids fluttered open. He could make out faces—Lucie, Lizzie, Jarvis Lorry, Miss Pross. A pale dawn light surrounded them. *Where am I?* he wondered. His ears made out the sound of horses' hooves and coach wheels. He felt heavy wool cloth against the fur of his neck and his four legs. He glanced down. He was wearing a tan coat—someone else's coat. *Sydney's coat! Why am I wearing Sydney's coat? Why is it dawn again? Dawn . . . my loved ones . . . in a coach . . . wearing Sydney's coat . . .*

All at once, Charles knew exactly what had happened. "No! No! Sydney! My friend! You're gone! Gone!"

Charles saw Lucie's face more clearly. Her blue eyes told him that she shared all his feelings—grief, horror, awe, joy, regret, relief. Each emotion was so powerful that he felt his heart would burst.

Charles lifted his front paws. Lucie clasped one to her lips. He could feel her tears fall on it. Lizzie held his other paw against her cheek. Miss Pross laid her hand on his furred forehead. Mr. Lorry grasped his shoulder. They sat that way as the sun came up, as it rose higher in the sky, as it shone down on them inside the coach.

No one said a word for hours. Finally Charles spoke. "Every minute that passes takes us farther from Paris and closer to London. But my thoughts never move. They stay with Sydney Carton—and I know they always will."

Chapter Nineteen

Great story! It makes me very sad and happy at the same time. I guess that's why it's great literature. I think Sydney Carton is one of the most honorable and courageous characters ever created by a writer.

In Oakdale, we have our own examples of honor and courage. Take Emily and Tina, for instance. When they saw Joe leading me off to the back porch, they showed their true colors.

"Wait!" Emily said.

David and Ellen turned to look at her. Joe and Wishbone hurried back into the living room from the kitchen.

"We did it," Emily confessed.

Tina nodded.

Ellen sounded puzzled. "Did what, honey?"

"The toilet paper," Emily said.

"And the juice in the kitchen," Tina added.

"Yes!" Wishbone did a somersault and leaped onto the couch next to Emily and Tina. "My case is now dismissed, thanks to you. It took courage to confess." He swatted the bow on his collar. "Now get this thing off of me."

Ellen bent down and untied the bow. "You're a good

dog, Wishbone. I'm sorry I blamed you." She rubbed the top of his head.

As usual, Wishbone's eyes half-closed with pleasure. "Nice, Ellen. Feel free to give me a reward, too—maybe one of those doggie ginger snaps."

Joe and David spent the next hour cleaning up the toilet paper and spilled juice. Emily drew a portrait of Wishbone, standing in profile. She gave it to him before she and Tina went home. Ellen taped the portrait to the refrigerator door—at just the right height for Wishbone to see.

That afternoon, after a nap and a snack, Wishbone sat in front of the refrigerator, admiring the portrait.

"I think Emily's got real talent. She captured a certain spirit, a certain *je ne sais quoi*—which is French for 'I don't know quite what.' Anyway, she got my good side."

Wishbone's ears pricked up. He heard footsteps—Ellen's and Joe's. A minute later, they both walked into the kitchen. They were wearing jackets. Joe was holding Wishbone's leash.

"We're going to the park, Wishbone," Joe said. "Come on, boy!"

Wishbone barked once, then followed them out the back door. "Yes! As Dickens said—it is the best of times! It is the spring of hope! Ah . . . we're not baby-sitting for anyone, are we?"

About Charles Dickens

Charles Dickens was born in 1812 in a town on England's southern coast. His family moved to London, where, in 1824, his father was sent to prison because of unpaid debts. Young Charles had to drop out of school to work in a blacking warehouse (blacking was a paste or polish used to dye objects such as leather). Because of his difficult experiences early in life, Dickens developed a deep concern for poor people. All his writing expressed outrage at the terrible conditions they endured.

At age fifteen, Dickens learned shorthand (a form of speed-writing). A few years later, he got a job reporting on debates in Parliament. He also began to write original stories for newspapers and magazines. In 1836–37, a series of related stories were collected in a book called *Pickwick Papers.* The series was a huge success. Soon publishers were clamoring for Dickens's work; famous people wanted to meet him; and fans begged for more stories.

Dickens wrote more than a dozen important novels (including *Oliver Twist, David Copperfield,* and *Great Expectations*). He had a true genius for creating unforgettable characters and gripping plots, and for portraying life in all parts of society. He quickly became the most popular writer of his time.

The energetic Dickens also edited magazines, gave public readings of his novels, and worked on amateur theater productions. He and his wife, Catherine, had ten children, but the marriage was not a happy one. Dickens died in 1870.

About *A Tale of Two Cities*

The idea for *A Tale of Two Cities* came to Charles Dickens while he was acting with his daughters and some friends in a play called *The Frozen Deep*, by Wilkie Collins. In the play, one man sacrifices his own life in order to rescue his rival and preserve the happiness of the woman they both love.

Dickens used this tiny "plot seed" to create a great historical novel about the French Revolution. A historical novel takes place in a period before the author's birth. It combines made-up characters and events with real ones from the past. Dickens wrote only two historical novels: *Barnaby Rudge*, published in 1841; and *A Tale of Two Cities*, in 1859.

In gathering background information, Dickens relied heavily on the writings of the famous nineteenth-century British historian Thomas Carlyle. Dickens also visited Paris many times. The beautiful city that Sydney Carton pictured at the end of the novel was the nineteenth-century Paris that Dickens knew and loved.

Dickens called *A Tale of Two Cities* "the best story I have written." In the book's preface, he declared, "Throughout its execution it has had complete possession of me." Some people claim this novel has the best-designed plot of all his books. It also contains two of his most powerful and unforgettable characters: Sydney Carton and Madame Defarge. Like so much of Dickens's work, *A Tale of Two Cities* makes readers aware of people's unnecessary suffering and the need for changes in society. But above all, it tells a terrific story—captivating, intense, and touching.

About Joanne Barkan

J oanne Barkan juggles two completely different writing careers. She is the author of more than one hundred children's books, including middle-grade fiction, non-fiction, stories for beginning readers, picture books, and preschool concept books. *Creatures That Glow*, her book about bioluminescence (light given off by animals such as glowworms and fireflies), won two science awards. *Anna Marie's Blanket*, a picture book, is a Children's Choices selection. For adults, she writes about politics and economics, and is a member of the editorial board of *Dissent* magazine. She likes writing for children and adults, but she recommends a double career only for people who enjoy having too much to do at once.

Barkan admits that, at age fourteen, she saw the Dirk Bogarde movie version of *A Tale of Two Cities* before she read the novel. She fell in love with the main character, Sydney Carton. Barkan immediately read Dickens's novel, then put it on her list of favorite books. The novel has special meaning for her because she studied in Paris for one year while in college, and she knows the city well.

She lives on the Upper West Side of Manhattan with her husband, Jon R. Friedman, a painter and sculptor. They like to go to modern dance performances, art museums, and movies. They also walk in Riverside Park almost every evening to watch the great gathering of pet dogs. Lately, Barkan looks out for Jack Russell terriers and asks their owners if they know Wishbone. They always do.